1440
812

HOSTAGE

HOSTAGE

A NOVEL

ELIE WIESEL

Translated from the French by Catherine Temerson

ALFRED A. KNOPF   NEW YORK   2012

THIS IS A BORZOI BOOK
PUBLISHED BY ALFRED A. KNOPF

A limited edition of this work is being published by Easton Press, Norwalk.

Library of Congress Cataloging-in-Publication Data
Wiesel, Elie, [date]
[Otage. English]
Hostage / Elie Wiesel ; translated from the French by Catherine Temerson.—1st ed.
p. cm.
ISBN 978-0-307-59958-2
1. Hostages—Fiction. 2. Kidnapping—Fiction. I. Temerson, Catherine. II. Title.
PQ268313208313 2012 843'.914—dc23 2011050747

Manufactured in the United States of America
First American Edition

Can man be free in prison? Can the eternal wanderer lose his sense of eternity as he gropes his way forward through the forest whose huge trees touch the sky? Will the child who is searching for the old man in order to gather his tears of joy and memories of sadness, find them before his years disappear in the mists of the grieving dawn?

Oh, if only I knew the art of questioning.

ONE-EYED PARITUS, "Time, a Series of Errors?"

HOSTAGE

"Someone is missing," Shaltiel murmurs, his head slightly tilted. No one has heard him.

Around the table, in the dining room, the guests are telling each other stories both related and unrelated to the circumstances uniting them that evening. The atmosphere is warm and joyous. How could it not be? Didn't they come to celebrate the life of a man and the freedom of men?

Policemen and intelligence agents, Americans and Israelis, friends and members of Shaltiel's family, they all feel they are entitled to it, to this privilege. They all suffered along with him, from close or from far away, often in secret; they all shared his anguish, or at least they were aware of it and it had left its mark.

"L'Chayim," says a big, bespectacled man with delicate hands as he raises his glass: "To life." And they all join in. Yes, to life. To the right to life. Everyone's right. To the joy of being with someone who was going to lose his life for unacceptable, absurd reasons.

Shaltiel runs his eyes over his friends, new and old. He is grateful to them all.

But someone is missing.

That's the way it is and I can't do anything about it.

Though I was surely born in joy, I have always lived in anguish.

In the basement, his thoughts catapult him into the past. So is this what a man's life is all about? Moving from one shelter to another, both opening out on brutality, remorse and nothingness?

It's only a dream, Shaltiel says to himself. An idiotic, senseless dream. As all dreams are. Inevitable and useless. Sometimes, we dream because we are anxious, and because we don't understand.

I am walking in the mountains. In the midst of a crowd. I am moving forward with slow steps. I don't know anyone. I have no idea why a strange instinct urges me to flee. Could the enemy be everywhere? I ask one person, then another: "What are we doing here?" A bearded old man replies: "It's you I'm looking for." He vanishes. A sad, dark-haired young woman replies: "It's you who are waiting for me." She vanishes too. A man with a gentle face says: "It's you." They all assert: "It's you." Behind them—it's odd—a stranger with an intense gaze nods his head and flashes a knowing wink at me; I know he's dead, but he's walking with the others. And he says nothing. Suddenly my heart starts pounding madly: They've all vanished, except the dead person, and that's me. I'm alone. And the mountains narrow in on me; they become me. And in my dream, I say to myself: It's a dream. Is it mine? Not theirs? How am I to know?

Oh, to unravel the fabrics of dreams and fantasies that inhabit the prisoner, to disentangle the time and duration that engross philosophers, the conscience of the ascetic and the intuition of psychologists, the fire and anathema of moralists so they won't turn into illusions and lies. Tell me, how is it done?

He is afraid: If he shuts his eyes, he plunges back into an unreal universe with people alive or dead. When he reopens them, the fear has not left him.

He remembers the pitch-black darkness, with red glimmers bearing misfortune, the sadness vying with astonishment; and, in the dream, his eyes fill with tears.

Who will speak of the role of fear in the torment experienced by the hostage who, on the level of fate or the gods, exists only for his executioners?

This tragedy, the very first of its kind, took place in 1975. It caused a considerable stir in the media at the time, in Jewish communities and in so-called diplomatic circles.

Shaltiel Feigenberg, a discreet man with no status or fortune, became famous all over the world.

But not for long.

Who remembers him today?

The buzzing in the ears.

The taste of ash.

The turmoil in my chest, the knot in my throat. The heart-rending feelings and thoughts.

Like before? In a different way, possibly worse. Before, over there, the danger threatened us all. Here it feels like I'm the only target.

It's the first day. Long, too long. Longer and longer. With few outside events. Where am I? In a large underground storage room? In a basement haunted by unspeakable villainies and curses? There are two bizarre individuals, their faces poorly concealed under hoods. Eventually they'll remove them. Nowadays that would no longer be possible: Terrorists are determined to remain anonymous. In regaining consciousness, my first sensation was the pain in the nape of my neck. There was blood in my mouth. Few words were exchanged: name, address, telephone number. Surely they already knew the answers.

"Where am I?"

"Far away," said a singsong voice.

"Who are you?"

"Your fate," said the same voice.

Could this be some sort of prank, young students in search of thrills or the sensational? This is all unthinkable. Peaceful, innocent citizens aren't supposed to be abducted.

They're making a mistake, Shaltiel said to himself. They think I'm someone else. That's the only possible explanation.

They think I'm lying to them. That I'm not me but one of their
enemies. Could a person's identity be a mistake, an accident?
A fatality? Freedom, a mental exercise? The life of a man, a
sham? Sages compare it to a leaf trembling in the wind, a fleet-
ing dream, the shadow of a bird or a cloud. Fine, as a moral
warning that's acceptable. But a cruel farce? Decided by whom?
For what purpose?

What do they want from me? What have I done to them?
Why are they bullying me so relentlessly?

"Whom do you know, among your Jewish friends, who's
rich and important? Talk, you fool, otherwise you're dead! The
Prophet's sword is merciless! Names, give us names! Out with
them! Jews, damn them, know influential people everywhere."

Insults, curses, spit. But no blows, not yet.

The mental suffering, the violation of my inner world—
why so much suffering once again?

Who are they? Who am I to them?

I don't understand, I don't understand a thing.

He passes a seemingly endless night. Crouched on the
floor, sleep escapes him. A few interruptions, a few starts, more
dreams and phantasmagorical visions: He is in a glass coach,
drawn by several white horses, singing and drifting in a fierce
wind toward massive mountains. Suddenly he realizes that children with petrified eyes have replaced the majestic horses.

What does that mean?

And this imprisonment, this isolation, what could they possibly mean? It's all a large, diabolical chessboard.

Hungry? Not at all. Thirsty, yes. Very thirsty. And so
exhausted that thinking seems impossible.

No doubt it is daybreak somewhere, for the noises from the

outside are becoming more audible—the roar of cars, the calls of children.

So we're close to a city. My guess is a suburb. As in the past? "Over there," the danger came from outside, and no one would interfere. Here, who knows? Perhaps someone will notice something odd.

Oh yes, and the police. The police: the eyes and ears of any civilized community. Blanca must have told them.

Patience. Advice to my nerves: Be strong. To my heart: Calm down. And to my brain: Don't panic. All of this will soon be solved. Tomorrow life will be beautiful.

Today starts off badly, though, with the first genuine cross-examination.

Shaltiel's words are pitiful, mutilated, forced out painstakingly and grudgingly. He already knows that it's been hours—long, sluggish hours—that he hasn't been free. He's been made a prisoner by strangers. Once again he is the victim of barbarity, but for what reason?

Deadened, assailed, his temples ache. Soon blood is going to flow, and will not stop. Can one drown in one's own blood?

"Don't be stubborn. You can't fight destiny. We're stronger than you. You'll come to a bad end."

"Where am I?"

"Far away."

"Who are you?"

"Your masters," says a harsh voice. "Your life is in our hands."

"Why?"

"Because it is," says another voice, less harsh.

"When will you let me go?"

"When we win the war," says the first voice, sniggering.

Restless children, elderly dreamers, the gods of love, his ungovernable demons, they are all swirling around in his throbbing head. Will he never again encounter them in freedom?

"But what do you want from me? Believe me! I swear on my own head, I don't understand, I don't . . ."

In the past, Shaltiel says to himself, a pious adolescent, I would have known what to do: I would have followed tradition and asked to establish a small *Bet Din,* a three-man court. I would have told them about my bad dream and they would have exorcised it by repeating the ritual incantation three times, "The dream you had is good, is good," wishing me peace, happiness, maybe forgetfulness and everything else.

That was the past. Here, I don't know anyone, except the angel of horror; he wears the mask of the executioner.

Where are Shaltiel's loyal friends?

As if to tear himself away from the present, he recalls Nathanael's story. Why him? Why not. When a tale comes to mind, there is no dismissing it.

It's like the story from his childhood, far away from here. The story he had been told: Once upon a time, in a small Romanian or Hungarian town, depending on the period, or the fantasy of the rulers, there was a little Jewish boy living alone for several weeks in a Christian family. It was during the war. He was still alive, he said to himself, thanks to Ibolya, a blond and mischievous little girl of about ten. She had discovered him in the fields, asleep, famished and lost. She ran to fetch her mother, Piroshka, a flamboyant redhead with sparkling eyes. Mother and daughter brought him home, to a house on the edge of the forest. The father was at the Russian front. They called the little refugee Sàndor, but his real name was Nathanael: gift of God. Later, Shaltiel was to see him in a Jewish school in Brooklyn.

A dream that brings on dreams?

Jewish memories. Each more painful and scalding than the next, bound together and tightened by the same fist that points the way to shadows, silent and distorted by anguish. Shaltiel relives them and shudders, a lump in his throat.

His head is full of images of a boy, still young, who has feelings of embarrassment, even remorse, about growing up; words, dreams, sobs, stories, more or less muddled. In Europe, he cultivated them. In New York too. His father, Haskel, a peddler of old books and ancient documents in Brooklyn, wasn't always at home; he was too busy trying to sell his merchandise, which the rich didn't want and the poor couldn't afford. His stepmother worked in other people's houses. As a ten-year-old, Shaltiel spent his days in school, but he didn't get to sit at the table with the other schoolboys; he sat apart, because the teacher felt the new immigrant was too young to learn to read the Aramaic texts, much less assimilate them.

But he learned them. By heart. In a low voice, cautiously, he would repeat what the tutor said, singing to himself: what

Rabbi Akiba said, what Rabbi Ishmael replied. Hillel's disciples said one thing, Shammai's, usually obstinate, said another. The chess player within him, even at so young an age, was of great assistance in remembering and foreseeing their thoughts.

When the students had their snack, Shaltiel made do with a bowl of milk given to him by the tutor's wife. One day, I'll have buttered bread, which I'll share with everyone, the child said to himself. And my father will be happy. And he'll no longer be exhausted. This thought was enough to buoy him up in his solitude.

The evenings, when he could spend them by his father's side, were a time of joy. Shaltiel admired and loved his father. To calm his son's hunger, the father gave him almost everything he received. Actually, he was never hungry when they were together.

The best time for Shaltiel was when his father and he played chess, their mood serious and attentive. Both were anxious not to make an irreparable mistake. Shaltiel also liked it when his father talked him to sleep at night. He talked about everything, even about Shaltiel's dead mother. The father would listen to his son recite his bedtime prayer and watch him sleep. The child, though, only pretended to sleep. He liked to feel his father's gentle gaze caress his face. He felt it to the edge of drowsiness, while in his head he went over the chess games that were yet to be resolved. Over there, far away, he sometimes wondered whether God, on high, wasn't playing chess with someone too, but with whom? Now that's the great question.

Some weeks Shaltiel saw him only on the Sabbath. Exhausted by his trips, Reb Haskel would run to the *Mikveh* for his ritual ablutions, purifying himself so as to welcome the sublime Sabbath Queen fittingly. He was no longer the same man. His whole being would glow with a secret, beneficial light.

Together, hand in hand, united by ties that seemed indestructible, father and son went to a Hasidic shrine for the service. Along the way, his father asked him his usual question: "What have you done with your days and evenings during this whole past week, my dearly beloved son?"

"I listened."

"Whom did you listen to?"

"Reb Moshe-Hayim the Melamed, the tutor."

"What did he say?"

"He said that our Sages not only knew how to express themselves well, but also how to listen well."

"What else?"

"He said that God also listens, but He alone understands."

Proud and happy, the father stroked his son's head and said: "Remember that's the most important lesson you'll have learned in life."

"Why?"

"Because, with it, you'll be able to build palaces in time and cultivate gardens in your mind."

And, after a silence, "Do you know, my son, that God conceived and created the world with twenty-two letters? And not just the visible world, but scores of others that aren't visible. Later, you'll learn about their power. Each one represents a superior and inflexible force. When you know how to assemble some of them, according to established but obscure rules, you'll be powerful and victorious."

Shaltiel kept his father's words inside him. He knew they were true. With his father by his side, he feared and envied no one. Returning home on Friday nights, his father was radiant: He put aside his worries about health or money. The three candles on the table, one for each member of the family, the wine for the Kiddush, the two braided breads so skillfully and lovingly prepared by Malka, his stepmother—Shaltiel lived all week long for these moments. It didn't matter that the meal was meager; it brought the three of them together at the same table, sometimes with his cousin Arele, savoring the little they had, united by a love that made their hearts glow. What more could they want?

Haskel and Malka were exhausted by their week's work, but it didn't show on their faces. They liked to linger at the table. They told each other about the events of the week. They talked about Haskel's customers, both the generous and the heartless ones. In one place, he would have been welcomed with a smile, though he might have left empty-handed; in another, he was greeted with the door slammed in his face. Haskel talked about the well-to-do families who sometimes didn't realize they were humiliating him. He didn't complain. Such is the mystery of the Sabbath: Joy predominates. Haskel and his nieces, Koli and Ahuva, when they were together, sang the appropriate songs. On occasion, they would ask Shaltiel to sing alone. And he would think: Thank you God for being God. And for having given us the most beautiful gift, the Seventh Day, so different from the others, a day whose peacefulness makes the trees and the stars in the sky sing.

The only anguish of the Sabbath was watching it slip away.

Somewhere, in an ancient Hasidic work lent to him by his father, he had read that at the Rabbi's court, during the Third Meal, tinged with melancholy, they implored the Lord to slow the rhythm of time, to suspend it, since the parting from the

Sabbath was so painful. It heralds the return of the everyday with its dangers and fears. Everywhere, men and children were hoping Mother or Grandmother was not in a rush, that she still had time to recite "*Gott fun Avrohom,*" "God of Abraham," the song of farewell to the Sabbath, that she could extend the peacefulness for a few more minutes—the sun had not yet set at the glowing red horizon.

Like his son, Haskel looks out the window to see if three stars are shining in the firmament, signifying that the holy day has ended. Day and night battle for the last rays of the sun. The young Shaltiel, with his naïve and poetic imagination, is convinced that the presence and departure of the Sabbath depend on his father, on the songs he sings in a strong or halfhearted voice, that his father's power is immense.

As soon as the evening prayer is finished, father and son hurry home to light the candles that separate the sacred from the profane and Israel from other nations. And they wish each other "Good week, good week." Let it be good for each of them. But, Shaltiel thinks, how could it really be good as they will not be together? From morning to night, his father will knock at the doors of hardhearted strangers, and he, Shaltiel, will be isolated at school from the boys luckier than he, listening to the tutor or imagining an invisible chessboard.

Later on, he will find the word describing his state of mind: exile. That is what he is all week, torn away from his parents, an unpopular exile who arouses uneasiness everywhere, and who drags his anguish along with him. A vague anguish, elusive, pernicious, imperceptible but all-consuming. Stifling. Worse: demeaning.

In school, at first, people made fun of young Shaltiel. They teased him and tried to provoke him. They had no compunctions about hurting him.

Months went by, but he remained solitary, powerless. More than the others, he suffered from the cold in the winter and the heat in the summer. Some classmates occasionally wore new clothes for the holidays. Not he. Often a scapegoat, he didn't take part in games, and didn't laugh with the others when one of them acted stupidly or insolently. He was unconnected.

Then, one day, he made a friend.

He must have been entering his eleventh or twelfth year. That day, Reb Haskel had fallen ill. Shaltiel (or Shalti, as his relatives called him) wanted to stay by his bedside, but Haskel wouldn't hear of it.

"A boy's place is in school," he ruled.

With a heavy heart, Shaltiel could only obey. In school, he could think only of his father. For the first time in his life, he didn't listen to what was being said around the long, rectangular table.

It was winter. The streets of Brooklyn were covered with icy patches buried under snow. As though grieving, the city breathed in slow motion. The skyscrapers were wrapped in mist, in a hush.

That day, the students were studying the Treatise on Punishments in the Talmud and, in the Bible, the chapter where the young Joseph, hated by his jealous brothers, is cast into a pit filled with snakes and scorpions. In tears, he implores his enemy brothers to get him out. Impervious to his pain and fear, they sit down to calm their hunger. The tutor waxed indignant: "How is this possible? Isn't it a disgrace? Joseph is suffering and crying, and his brothers think only of their stomachs? And after that, what do they do? They sell him into slavery! He, son of Jacob, grandson of Isaac and great-grandson of Abraham! It is hardly surprising that in the Talmud our Sages, blessed be their memory, declare that day as one of the darkest in the history of our people! They sold him for a bit of money and shoes!"

At that point Shaltiel could not hold back his tears. The tutor noticed him for the first time, really, and congratulated him: "You're crying for the unfortunate Joseph, that's good. This shows you have a good heart—not like all those idlers sitting here."

And so the other students glared at Shaltiel, as though it were his fault that Joseph's brothers had behaved contemptibly. He felt their annoyance. He himself was surprised by the words he blurted out: "No, I'm not crying for Joseph. I'm crying for my father. He's unwell, and there's no one at home to take care of him."

The students stared at him, some with astonishment, others with compassion.

"What's wrong with your father?" asked the tutor, fondling his beard.

"I don't know," Shaltiel replied. "He's sick. So sick that he stayed home."

A silence fell over the children as if to punish them.

"Go home," said the tutor, in a tone that was now charitable. "Your father needs you more than we do. Tell him it's my decision, not yours. You'll come back tomorrow."

Shaltiel went home. Haskel didn't hide his joy. As Malka was at work, he asked his son to make him tea. Then he fell asleep.

The next day, at school, Shaltiel was given a seat at the table. When it was his turn to read the text, Shaltiel had good diction and knowledge that no one suspected. The tutor and the schoolboys were all taken aback.

"Where did you learn to read the text and the commentaries of Rashi and the Tosafists?" the tutor asked.

"Right here," Shaltiel answered.

"No one at home helped you?"

"No one. When my father isn't ill, he's away all week."

"How did you do it?"

"Well, I have a good memory. It comes in handy when you play chess too."

The tutor looked at him for a long time before smiling.

"It takes a lot to astonish me. But you did. And I'm grateful to you."

Nathanael, the top student in the class, drew close to Shaltiel. And so the friendship was born.

This was such a long time ago.

Did I live, did I survive, for this? Shaltiel wondered. To lose my freedom, my right to happiness? I know the power of the irrational on the course of events, but why does it so often turn out to be harmful? From one minute to the next, everything changes. You breathe in another way. You hope for something different. One minute of respite is a blessing. Memories become a great help.

His world had shrunk to the size of a basement.

When I was freed, I found out that at home, when the sun went down, my family didn't know what to make of my disappearance. Usually I liked to watch the spectacle of the sunset with children and old people, and invent stories for them. "Enter here," I said to them, "enter into my story, the one we may be living through and that I bring to life," incantatory words like stifled cries responding to men's heartbeats, to the wounds of the earth. As they listened, the children became sadder, the old men did not; they simply hoped for the sun's return.

Why my unexpected absence? I will recall the facts. All this took place three years after the murder of the Israeli athletes at the Munich Olympics, one year before the Israeli Entebbe rescue operation, and well before the abductions and suicide murders that are so common nowadays. In those days, when someone disappeared in the United States, one didn't assume the worst. But my family was worried. Where could I possibly be? With whom? My wife, Blanca, and our two nieces, Koli and Ahuva, who lived more often with us than at Malka's sister's house, first thought it was due to my absentmindedness. They presumed I had gotten lost, because I always have had problems with schedules and geography. Whenever we set off to see friends or went to the supermarket, they poked gentle fun at me: If I said "Right," then it had to be to the left. Whenever we made an appointment to meet at the theater, I always made the appointment early, for fear of arriving late. Koli thought I was merely late. Ahuva, a redhead, replied: "No, he probably got lost." Koli said, "Or went to the wrong city." "No," said Blanca, "you know Shalti: He makes two appointments at the same time, in two different places."

The dinner ready, the table set, they were waiting only for me. Finally, Blanca decided to call Grandfather first. Did he know where I could be at so late an hour without giving a sign of life? Then she called the local library, then close friends.

Everyone said the same thing: "We haven't seen him since." As time went by, all three stood at the window looking down on the street, increasingly filled with anxiety. "He's never done anything like this before," Blanca said. "Something must have happened to him." Koli suggested calling the police. Ahuva said they should call local hospitals. They decided it was best to call the local police precinct.

Blanca: My husband is very late in coming home. We're very worried.

The policeman: His name?

Blanca: Shaltiel Feigenberg.

The policeman: His profession?

Blanca: Storyteller. He gives talks in the community.

The policeman: Did you say storekeeper or storyteller?

Blanca: Storyteller.

The policeman: Is that a profession?

Blanca: He says it's more like a calling.

The policeman: Maybe he fell asleep in his office?

Blanca: He has no office. He works at home.

The policeman: A girlfriend?

Blanca: What? I don't know what to say. I can't imagine it . . .

The policeman: Okay, okay. Sometimes that's the simple explanation. I guess not in this case. I will do a little research. If you have no news in the next few hours, call us back.

The two girls wanted to know why Blanca had lost her temper on the phone. "I'm like your uncle. I don't like rude people who, because they have a bit of power, think they can get away with anything," she answered.

Blanca and Koli went to police headquarters, where their anxiety was taken more seriously. (Ahuva stayed home to answer the phone, just in case.) The scene was chaotic, but they found their way to the missing persons department. A polite officer, in his early forties, with a mustache, greeted them professionally.

"First, the good news. Your husband isn't on any of our victim lists. He hasn't been attacked, fallen off a bus or suffered a heart attack in the middle of the street. Could he have gone for a walk by the sea? Or gone to relax in a swimming pool?"

"My husband doesn't swim."

"And I assume you've contacted all your relatives, friends and relations?"

"Yes."

"Could he be working on a project that requires a meeting, an unforeseen trip?"

"No. Let me explain. His projects are in his head. He's knight of the imaginary, a magician of the word. He sometimes goes out for a bit of air or, as he says, to talk to the birds so he can better interpret their chirping, but it's never for long. If he's going to be late, he always warns me."

"And today?"

"He might have gone to the library this morning. He came home for lunch. Then he went out again."

"For what reason?"

"Sometimes he works better when he walks."

Koli added, "And also when he talks to children."

"What children?" asked the officer.

"Any children. When he sees a sad child in the street, he

wants to hear his story, to learn from him and to drive away the child's sadness."

"And then? Does he try to see him again?"

"No. Never. My husband has only one obsession: fantasy. He has seen and lived through too many of the world's sorrows and bereavements, you understand; he believes it's his mission to side with those who suffer, to tell their stories. The deprived, disoriented children."

"Where does he find these children?"

"Anywhere. In poor neighborhoods. In schools. In parks. But once he knows their stories he never tries to see them again."

"Kind of odd," the policeman says.

"He does the same thing with old people."

"A peculiar kind of guy."

The officer finished what he was writing and looked up.

"What can I say except don't worry too much? It often happens that men or women of a certain age feel a sudden need to break away from their social, family or professional environment, for a day and sometimes longer. This doesn't mean anything. They almost always return home. I advise you to wait it out. As for us, we'll do some research. I give you my word: We'll bring your husband back to you, safe and sound."

Blanca and Koli returned home. Ahuva met them with the news that there had been no telephone call.

Blanca had already called her in-laws, Haskel and Malka. She called them again. Shaltiel hadn't showed up. Sometimes he would drop in on them unexpectedly, just to kiss them or to tell them that everything was okay in his little family. Blanca tried to hide her fear that something alarming had happened. In vain. Pessimistic by nature, her in-laws couldn't help dreading the worst. "Won't it ever end?" Malka said. She didn't make it clear what she meant by "it." No need to. Both she and Haskel were survivors.

They seldom mentioned their experiences "over there," in the cursed universe where Death and Evil substituted for man's Creator and Judge. When Haskel was questioned, he answered that, in order to give an answer, a new language would have to be invented. Malka felt the same way. If you wanted a piece of information or comment on that subject, you would have to force the words out of Haskel. Shaltiel agonized over this. How was he to prevent his father and stepmother from taking almost all their past silently with them to the grave?

In the past few years, Haskel had been teaching in a Hebrew seminary and Malka had obtained a part-time job in a Jewish nursery school. They never complained: "Jews like us have no right to," they said. In contrast to what they had been subjected to, they blessed their luck and considered themselves relatively fortunate. They were happy to work, happy to have started a family, happy to be alive, or rather to have survived.

Haskel had been deported from Transylvania to Auschwitz and Malka from Lithuania to Ravensbrück. They met in a camp for displaced persons in Germany at the end of the war. They fell in love and married. An American military rabbi officiated at the wedding ceremony, in the presence of Shaltiel, Arele and some strangers. Their honeymoon lasted one day. It was the rabbi who helped them immigrate to America.

Coming back to the present: "If Shaltiel is neither in prison nor in the hospital," said Malka, "it's a bad sign. I wonder if our enemies aren't involved."

She saw enemies everywhere.

"Which ones?" asked Blanca.

"I have no idea. Probably the same ones as in the past. They'll never give up."

Haskel kept silent on the other end of the phone, but Blanca, clinging to a tenuous and vague hope, took the liberty of contradicting her mother-in-law.

"This isn't Hitler's Europe. In those days, you couldn't ask the police to protect you from the enemy because the police were the enemy. Today, here, you can. The police are going to help us."

"I prefer to put my trust in God," said Malka.

A few minutes later, Blanca received a call from the abductors, plunging her into sadness and uncertainty.

The hours drag on, heavy with anxiety. Shaltiel, in his delirium, becomes more and more pessimistic. He says to himself that whereas in the first basement he used to pass the time by playing chess in his head, here, in the second one, he feels even dirtier and more diminished, virtually repudiated by life, and his only meager comfort is talking to the shadows. It is before them that he wonders about the meaning of this adventure. To them, he talks about his secrets.

Of course Shaltiel is ignorant of the developments that his disappearance has led to. As soon as Blanca, dry-eyed and determined, had relayed the abductors' message to the police, the police commissioner, John Ryan, a rock-solid Irishman, made her sit down in his office. He then called Saul, his deputy in charge of antiterrorist activities in the metropolitan area, who joined them.

Saul, a Brooklyn native, had been recruited from the FBI. In his forties, athletic-looking and elegant, he had a piercing gaze behind his horn-rimmed glasses. He was an intelligent man, with a sober, calm dynamism. He avoided the media, so few people knew of him.

Three hours earlier, Blanca told them, about 10:30 p.m., the telephone rang in her apartment. A voice whispered, "Don't wait up for your husband. He's in our hands. We'll put him on trial for his crimes against the Palestinian people. We demand that three of our soldiers be freed. One is in America; the other two are in Israel. If our demand is rejected, your husband will be executed. We must have an answer tomorrow."

Her hands on her lap, Blanca fell silent with a blank stare.

"He gave no specific time?" Ryan asked.

"No."

"No name?" asked Saul.

"No name."

"Not even the names of the prisoners?"

"No names at all."

She remembered one detail. "The caller had a European accent."

"Was it German perhaps?" Saul asked. He had hunted down Nazis in the past.

"No. A singsong accent. French or Italian."

"Are you sure?" asked the commissioner.

"Yes," said Blanca.

Without being asked, Blanca handed Ryan some photos of Shaltiel. The two officials thanked her and questioned her about her husband—his work, his passions (children and the elderly), his habits (Jewish ritual, reading, walks), his friends and acquaintances. Was he involved in politics? No. Did he sometimes take part in pro-Israeli demonstrations? Never. It wouldn't be like him. Does he drink? Does he ever use, hmm, undesirable substances? Was he ever away for such a long period of time before? Did she suspect he had a girlfriend?

Blanca, inured to any potential offense by now, answered all these questions as best she could.

"We'll do everything we can to bring your husband back," said Ryan. "But for the time being, you should keep all this to yourself; it's in his best interest, and yours, and ours too. If it gets out, the media will pick up the story. And inevitably things will get more complicated."

She nodded and left.

The photos of Shaltiel were sent immediately to the police and FBI labs.

"What do you make of this business?" the commissioner asked Saul.

"I don't like the looks of it," Saul said.

"I don't either."

"Interesting—they're not asking for money."

"Three prisoners, but they didn't give their names."

"They must be Arab."

"There are several in our jails."

An emergency meeting was called within the hour for all the members of the antiterrorist unit. Ryan gave them a quick rundown of the situation. Then each was given an assignment and a schedule was drawn up. From that day on, until Operation Storyteller came to an end, the higher officials were to meet twice a day.

In a matter of hours, Shaltiel Feigenberg became the focal point of dozens, and soon hundreds, of law enforcement personnel. His photo, thousands of copies of which were made, would attract the attention of train station and airport employees, gas station attendants and even casino habitués. But no mention was made of abduction.

The first results were disappointing. One person remembered running into him in front of a newspaper stand. Another recalled seeing a fifty-year-old who looked like him entering a flower shop and never coming out. One employee at a train station remembered selling him a ticket to Washington, D.C.; another employee said he had sold him a ticket to Chicago. It didn't take long before a journalist phoned the police commissioner to obtain additional information about the missing person. Ryan took an unusual step in requesting his silence; once it was given, Ryan informed him of the broad outlines of Shaltiel's abduction. When other journalists inquired, Ryan went to their bosses to request their cooperation. They all wanted to know if he was hiding more substantial information; he swore that he was not. For the time being, they knew as much about what had happened as he and his subordinates. He asked them to promise not to release any new detail they might come upon. Each promised, so long as all the others agreed to do the same.

He told them he would keep them informed.

Ryan instructed Saul to call the State Department. "They can get information from the Israel Ministry of Foreign Affairs about the possible Arab terrorists who might be involved in this business," he said.

Saul returned after only a few minutes.

"They're already informed. We'll have the names in a few hours. They don't think Israel will free anyone. And we won't either. Looks like Mr. Feigenberg will be going through a bad period."

Actually, for Shaltiel Feigenberg, things were already going badly, very badly.

Just as in the past. And then too it was in a basement.

Hours went by and the New York police made no progress. Six detectives were working on the case nonstop, checking through the archives, questioning their sources in the Mafia and in Muslim circles. They didn't come up with one lead.

By mid-afternoon several meetings had been called and many reports filed. Saul had met all of Shaltiel's relatives and friends in the area. They consented to having their telephone lines wiretapped. Security forces in several countries were alerted in case the hostage was no longer on American soil.

The abductors contacted Blanca again—three twenty-second phone calls from two different telephone booths, detailing their demands and giving instructions. Their words were few and carefully chosen. There were two voices, one Arabic-inflected, one not. The ultimatum was extended to three days hence. If their demands weren't met—in other words, if their comrades in arms were not free in three days—the hostage would be executed.

During the third call they gave the names of those to be released: Hassan Idris, Mahmed Yussuf and Rashid Moussa. The first two were in Israeli prisons; the last one, sentenced three months earlier as an accessory to murder, was awaiting the appeal of his case in a maximum-security prison in the United States.

When Saul heard about the calls, he asked to see the prisoners' records.

Ryan told Saul that he had talked to Dan Ramati, head of Mossad. "Dan confirmed what we already knew. Jerusalem sticks to its political principle of never giving in to terrorist blackmail. He said he was going to send us one of his best agents as a consultant. Did you hear from him yet, Saul?"

"Yes," Saul said. "His name is Hagai. He'll be coming with Rachel, his deputy. Hagai sounds like a real professional, though he's young. He thinks things will turn very sour if we don't soon find where the hostage is being held. Rachel evidently has been involved in lots of secret operations in Arab countries. She's very charming."

"Will Israel allow us to negotiate the abductors' demands?" Ryan asked.

"Ramati doesn't think so. The Israeli government insists on our taking a united stand. As you said, they won't give in to terrorists. If you show you're weak once, soon you'll have more of the same."

A detective eavesdropping asked, "Even if it's to save the life of a Jewish hostage?"

"Ramati would like to get permission to bring over his entire unit from Tel Aviv to take part in our investigation," Saul said.

"That's like admitting that we can't manage on our own," said the detective.

"Calm down," said Ryan. "These guys have helped us more than once. In any case, nothing will be done without the approval of the White House. And Jerusalem."

"How about inviting Ramati to our meeting tomorrow?" asked Saul.

"Good idea. He's not one of us; his impressions could be useful. What bothers me is that we're not getting anywhere."

A policeman arrived with the records of the three prisoners. "All three are Palestinian," he said. "The one here is from Hebron. He was arrested for aiding and abetting a homicide, illegal gun possession and for being a member of an underground terrorist group. The two in Israel are from Gaza; they were arrested during an attack on a civilian bus not far from Tel Aviv."

Ryan wanted their families contacted.

"What if the identities are fake," Saul asked.

"Let's find out."

Agence France Presse,

OCTOBER 24, 1975

The security services in New York have been mobilized after the disappearance of Shaltiel Feigenberg, an
American citizen born in Europe. Sources report a connection to ongoing violence in the Middle East.

The New York Times,

OCTOBER 24, 1975

. . . unofficial sources confirm that the missing man
lives in Brooklyn. The police refuse to release more
detailed information, other than to say that he is the
son of a Holocaust survivor.

Associated Press,

NEW YORK, OCTOBER 24, 1975

. . . the New York police in charge of investigating the
disappearance of Shaltiel Feigenberg refuse to specu-
late on whom the abductors might be and what their
demands are.

Yedioth Ahronoth,

TEL AVIV, OCTOBER 24, 1975

The government's top-level security cabinet held an
emergency session last night to discuss the disappearance of Shaltiel Feigenberg in the United States. The
prime minister reminded his colleagues of the tradi-

tion that all his predecessors have abided by: to consider themselves responsible for the life and security of
endangered Jews everywhere in the world, including in
friendly countries. The Israeli secret service has offered
its help to American law enforcement agencies . . .

So, from one day to the next, Shaltiel Feigenberg and his family became famous. Their names and faces appeared on the
front pages of newspapers. "The Mysterious Disappearance of
a Jewish Storyteller" was one headline. They were discussed on
television. President Gerald Ford, when brought up to speed,
made his concern publicly known. His secretary of state, Henry
Kissinger, followed developments closely. The prospective
presidential, senatorial and congressional candidates published
statements condemning "all forms of terrorism and proclaim-
ing their solidarity with the Jewish people." Blanca and her
nieces reluctantly submitted to the journalists' questions to
assuage them.

Time magazine quoted Malka saying that the investiga-
tions should focus on anti-Semitic groups: "It's simple. They're
everywhere. They won't forgive us for having survived and for
having children." (The magazine pointed out that the hostage
had no children.)

The New York Times published excerpts of a short story that
Blanca had found in the jumble of her husband's desk drawers.
A literary agent contacted her and asked whether she wouldn't
consider publishing his short stories in a book that could be
produced in a matter of weeks.

An Israeli evening daily printed Shaltiel's Israeli short story

in its entirety. It was hardly characteristic of his oeuvre, if oeuvre is the right word. It lacked the intellectual, let alone mystical, preoccupations of his other writings. This one was an
action narrative.

Brooklyn was in turmoil. Some young Hasidim created a small
self-defense group and offered to protect the Feigenberg family.
Their elders announced a day of fasting and invited the entire
community to join them in reciting the appropriate Psalms:
Heaven will help the Jews when men prove to be powerless or
indifferent. A great mystic spent the entire night in silence, in
strict reverent meditation, trying to locate and protect Shaltiel.

In Israel, for understandable reasons, official circles and the
public were following the Feigenberg episode with ever-greater
interest. Are people more interested in the fate of a writer, no
matter how modest, than in the fate of an anonymous person?
Possibly.

The special adviser to Prime Minister Yitzhak Rabin, General Peleg HarEven, summoned Dan Ramati. Tall, elegant, taut
with an angular face, looking perpetually curious and vigilant,
he was feared, dreaded and admired.

Ramati, who had been nicknamed "the great," had had a
legendary life. In his youth, before the creation of the Jewish
state, in the years 1942 to 1948, he had been a member of the
famous Berger Group, whose members were called terrorists
by their opponents and resistance fighters by their supporters.
The number two man on the English security services' most-

wanted list, he was reputed for carrying out bomb attacks. In the official structure of the state of Israel, as the director of the Mossad, he had exceptional authority, both professional and moral. His opinions were sought after and respected.

"What do you think of the Feigenberg case?" asked the prime minister.

"I don't know yet. I've sent two of our best people to New York. We have excellent relations with the FBI and the CIA, so that shouldn't be a problem."

"I want you to make this affair a priority. And to take charge of it personally."

"Why? Is there something here I'm unaware of?"

"No. But there *is* something that seems important to me, an intimate connection that has to exist between the Jewish state and the Jewish people—I mean, the Jewish Diaspora. This may be taking place in America, but I think we have a role to play in it. In my mind, wherever a Jew is threatened or persecuted just because he's Jewish, we're responsible for his fate. Keep me posted."

Dan Ramati nodded his head approvingly.

They are in a dilapidated, foul-smelling basement with a few odd chairs and overturned benches. A small window near the ceiling is full of dust and produces a cloudy beam of light. A smell of acrid smoke causes occasional sneezing. Huge cobwebs hang from the ceiling and fill the corners.

There are two men and their hostage. An Arab, Ahmed, is impatient and speaks with a guttural, nervous voice. An Italian, Luigi, seems more easygoing. His voice can be gentle, almost warm at times.

"What do you want from me?" Shaltiel asks. "What have I done to you? Why did you bring me here? Who are you? What am I to you?"

"We can be whatever you want us to be, your salvation or your death," says Ahmed. "Don't have any illusions: You can yell until hell freezes over; no one will hear you. And even if they do, no one will care about your fate. They'll write about you in the newspapers for a few days, then they'll forget all about you. We have three days left. If our demands aren't met, too bad for you."

Shaltiel can vaguely make them out through his ill-adjusted black blindfold. They're looking hard at him, as if they expect to see him change in some way. He can see their silhouettes. Odd, it's not like in the crime films where the prisoner can't see a thing. Is he dealing with amateurs or professionals?

He can distinguish half their faces, like masks. He sees huge eyes. I'm speaking to eyes, not human beings, Shaltiel thinks.

Somewhere in his subconscious, a voice keeps whispering: This must be a case of mistaken identity, a monumental, stupid mistake. These things happen. They must somehow think I'm a dangerous person. But I'm not a danger to anyone. He had been on his way to Srulik Silber's, an old collector friend, whose house, near the ocean, was crammed with books and esoteric manuscripts. It was an unplanned visit. Shaltiel was going home and suddenly felt like seeing Srulik, especially since he had to return an eighteenth-century Sabbatean pamphlet that he had borrowed the week before. He liked Srulik. Last month, Shaltiel was telling him that his erstwhile dreams had evaporated a long time ago. The Messiah would not be coming. The world, cursed through its own fault, would not be saved; the Messiah would arrive too late, or, as Kafka said, on the day after. Srulik smiled when Shaltiel said that. "Do you really think I don't know?" he asked.

He never got to meet Srulik again because Satan meddled. Footsteps came up behind him, someone was suddenly rushing, shadows were approaching. Shaltiel walked on, heedless. He was struck on the back of his neck and collapsed, his head on fire. As he regained consciousness, everything was swirling around. The stars were falling with a thunderous noise.

And what about the book he was going to return to Srulik, full of calculations sketched out in concentric circles? It was meant for the initiated and was particularly interesting. Why was everything being sabotaged by some curse plunging him into this makeshift prison?

There is an unpleasant half-light. He is *clinging*. At first, to pass the time, he plays mental chess against an imaginary opponent. If he wins, he thinks, God will smile down on him; he'll get his freedom back. But it's difficult. The white bishop makes a marvelous opening. The king is too old, too slow. The queen is too nimble, too quick, too eager to win. The knight is a prisoner. The game is interrupted by his torturers.

Timidly, a pale beam of sunshine infiltrates through the basement window, protected by two wooden bars. Is it daybreak or dusk?

"You're Jewish," says an Arab voice. "Your name is Shaltiel Feigen-something. Feigenberg, that's it. It's in your papers. Married. You're a peddler. What do you sell?"

"Words," says Shaltiel.

"You making fun of me?"

"No, it's the truth. I sell words."

"I don't believe you. No one buys words."

"They pay for my living."

How do they know these things about me? Shaltiel wonders. Oh yes, my documents. It's all listed. But then they surely know that I've done no harm to anyone and that I have no money. My wristwatch is worth all of twelve dollars. I don't get mixed up in things that are none of my business. I'm happy to have a few friends, who, like me, are in love with words and the silence between them. My life is of no consequence, except for my family. I don't understand what's happening to me.

"You want my poverty? You can have it."

"And he thinks he's funny," the Arab says as he laughs.

"Not so clever," the other one adds. "Do you think we don't know?"

"Well then . . ."

"Well then what? We know you're not rich. But we'll get something out of you, something that's not money. We're fighters in the Palestinian Revolutionary Action Group, and you're our prisoner."

"Why me? I'm not important. No one will satisfy your demands for my sake, you can be sure."

Then, in a neutral tone, with no sign of hatred, Luigi explains, as if to a student:

They're not looking for money; they couldn't care less about money. That they could get more easily and with less risk. Others give them money. They are interested in playing their part in the life and history of Islam. His organization decided to try to do on the American continent what his comrades are doing in other places, all over the Middle East. It's the first time. Yes, it's the first operation on American soil, which is supposed to be safe, secure, impregnable, according to the boasts of its leaders. Hostage taking is more profitable than ordinary attacks in Tel Aviv, Paris or London. It doesn't cost them anything in human lives and brings them worldwide publicity, as well as the liberation of their comrades-in-arms. So this is a new strategy of the radical Palestinians, faithful to their military, national and religious objectives. They are gambling on Jewish solidarity and taking advantage of its influence on Western governments.

At first, it all seemed unreal to Shaltiel, a crazy scheme staged by men obsessed with pointless, criminal violence.

The first night dragged by populated with predatory, threatening shadows. It's a tale, Shaltiel said to himself, a frightening tale, senseless and improbable, in which I'm both the witness and victim. It's a tale in which someone like me is tormented. It's not me who is aching, who is thirsty. I'm somewhere else. I live in another city, in another world. In another body, another story, another mystery, another person. Soon I'll wake up, find I'm intact and serene, impatient to string together words that make people dream.

All Ahmed knows is how to insult, swear and curse. He is playing the familiar part of the wicked inquisitor alongside the nice one. Drunk with frustration, he takes it out on his powerless victim. His favorite words are "done for." "You're done for, you're all done for, the Jews are done for," he says. In the first few hours, that's as far as he goes. Mental torture is enough for him. Everything about him spreads anger and hatred: hatred toward the Jewish state, the Jewish people, the Jewish past, the Jewish religion, Jewish money, Jewish power. These are his obsessions, his phobias, complete and all-enveloping. At least, this is the impression he wants to give. Every word coming out of his mouth is a gratuitous insult, an obscene swearword, a poisoned arrow or a call to suffering, humiliation, denial, murder.

In his view, the Jewish infidels will survive only so they can be punished by Allah and oppressed by his devoted servants. They are the cause of all evil weighing on the world. They are the incarnation of transgression, impurity personified, the vermin of the earth, society's cancer, the enemies of peace, the negation of happiness. Realizing that Shaltiel was guilty only of belonging to the accursed people, Ahmed quickly saw how he could take advantage of the situation: He had to coerce his hostage into signing a "voluntary" declaration condemning the Jewish state for "all the crimes committed against the unfortunate Palestinians." He also wanted to get him to request that men of goodwill, on every side of the political spectrum, save his life by obtaining the liberation of the three Palestinian "prisoners of war."

Between the obscenities punctuating the Arab's orders, Shaltiel finds himself regretting two things: that he never acquired the mystical powers that would make him invisible and that he never studied the Koran. Does the Muslim holy book, held to be sacred by countless believers, really preach bloodthirsty violence? His mind, molded by the study of Jewish sources, refuses to accept this. If the Koran represents contemporary Islam, as practiced by his abductors, he feels it is a religion much to be pitied.

Ahmed believes that he is the Prophet's personal servant. It is He who commands him to do what he does. Hence his conviction that he can do as he pleases. Shaltiel is his enemy and the enemy of his brothers in the desert; he must be denied pity. He must be crushed, his will shattered, his faith ridiculed, his honor sullied, his reason denounced, his dignity destroyed; he must be smashed, trampled on, his soul emptied of its powers and treasures. Ahmed's immediate goal is specific: compelling the masters in Tel Aviv and Washington to accept his political demands. In front of his implacable, inflexible determination, they will show themselves to be weak and cowardly. The key to his victory is here before him: this pathetic Yid, Shaltiel Feigen-whatever.

Little by little, Ahmed convinces himself that, in addition to the liberation of the Muslim prisoners, it will be essential for him to force the hostage to disown his people—those manipulators, renegades, criminal gangsters, children of the devil and death.

"Whether you admit it or not, from the fact of being Jewish, you've got Muslim blood on your hands," he says to his prisoner. "What the Jews are doing at home, they're doing in your name too."

"No, no, no!" protests Shaltiel, who hasn't yet understood the meaning of this accusation. "I'm Jewish, but I've never humiliated anyone. I've never committed a crime! You've made a mistake about me. I'm not the person you're looking for. I'm not your enemy! I'm against all humiliation, all persecution; I'm opposed to violence in every form, for violence includes violation. The Jew that I am, the storyteller I am, repudiates it with all my heart and soul."

Ahmed isn't listening to him. There is no discussing theology, sociology and politics when someone is under the spell of a self-enclosed totalitarian ideology. Intentionally or out of ignorance, Ahmed, who is empirical in all matters, detests pointless and laborious philosophical imaginings, never-ending discussions, or clashes of ideas that might be respectful of non-believer opponents and sinners deserving only of complete contempt. His argument boils down to two words: yes and no. His vocabulary is meager, limited to threats and swearwords. His role is not to listen but to be listened to. As he sees it, every infidel is a potential hostage. He is the all-powerful, omniscient master; the slave owes him not just absolute obedience, but also his existence and survival.

Even torture that is only verbal reinforces the power of the torturer: The prisoner's imagination leads him to dread the next round of interrogations. And when it happens, the feeling of inferiority becomes more acute; it bores into the brain, and the cultural and psychological defenses that surround the brain disintegrate and vanish. The ego is dissolved. Could Ecclesiastes be right? Is a living dog worth more than a dead lion? Chased from his throne by Ashmedai, the master of demons, good King Solomon, the wisest of men, experienced mental torments too. Physical pain comes later. For the tortured, all the knowledge acquired from childhood in the course of a lifetime won't protect you. The moans seem to issue from another body. In the end, the victim doesn't have anything or anyone to cling to. It's the feeling of falling into a bottomless well. Suddenly emptiness or the idea of emptiness appeals to him. Oh, to have an empty head, an empty heart, an empty future; to think of nothing, to feel nothing: This would be paradise in the middle of hell.

But Shaltiel knows this is impossible. His breath is not the only thing binding him to life. He has his parents, his wife, his close friends; they must be dying of anguish. What do they know? What are they doing? Who are they calling? What are the police doing? What is the press saying? In his imagination— and it fits with reality—he imagines Brooklyn in turmoil: the intense speculation in the study and prayer houses; the Hasidim consulting their Teacher, who advises them to recite particular Psalms. In her powerlessness, Blanca must be agonizing. If there is anyone who is moving heaven and earth, it is she. Nothing stops her; nothing holds her back. Dynamic and full of ideas, she must be running from one office to the next, from one of the dozens of Jewish organizations to another; he can hear her motivating them, encouraging them, urging them to act: Surely someone can get to a congressman, a government official.

"So, you little bastard Yid," Ahmed yells. "Are you going to open your filthy mouth finally? If you don't talk, I'll make you drink your own blood! Are you going to ask for the liberation of my heroic comrades? Are you going to sign a confession and publicize your disgust for the Jewish army and the Jewish politicians? They will be done for in time, I can guarantee that! And you first and foremost!"

Meeting with flat refusals, the Arab moved away and seemed to take his companion to task, as though he were testing his loyalty to their cause.

"We've got to get him to show his weakness and cowardliness publicly. Thanks to him, we'll force the liberation of my brother and the others and also gain the respect of revolutionaries throughout the world. That's our mission!"

So there are only two of them, thinks Shaltiel. Two men, two terrorists, bound by hatred. Yet, listening to them, they're so different. One will never change because he won't entertain doubts, but is the other one capable of doubting? In the end, which of the two will kill me? Actually, what's the difference. Inevitably, they'll go through with it.

He says to himself that like Dostoyevsky he'll be a witness to the preparations of his own execution.

He hears a door opening and closing. One of the terrorists has gone out. It's the Italian. Ahmed begins to manhandle his prisoner, hoping he'll reach a breaking point.

Shaltiel takes refuge in his memories and in words, as usual. He calls them, but they don't obey. Ideas and images overlap, become distorted, diverted, disassociated. Finally, a wave of panic turns to tenderness.

Suddenly, a weird thought pops into his head: Why not

make a "confession" and sign their preposterous statements, to which no intelligent person will attach any importance, and put an end to this stupid, horrendous spectacle? Other men, ever so much more influential than he, have done this, in another day and age: Nikolay Bukharin, Lev Kamenev, Zinovyev—great statesmen, illustrious generals, admired revolutionaries, former companions of Lenin—when their suffering became unbearable. He can't do it, though he could perhaps advise the Americans and the Israelis to liberate the three Palestinians, but he could not accuse Israel of war crimes or crimes against humanity: His own memory and that of his parents won't allow it. Yet it would be so simple: Saying yes under threat is not a disgrace. If he gave in, surely Jews would understand. Didn't he write articles supporting Jerusalem in an obscure Jewish monthly put out by the Department of Literary Studies at a Jewish college in Ohio? He used a Hebrew name, Shaltiel ben Haskel.

He suddenly finds himself trembling. Is it possible these Palestinian terrorists have read his articles and discovered the real name of their author? Perhaps his abduction was calculated. But why would they read a publication whose readership was so limited that it had to close down for lack of a subsidy? Yet in his feverish pain, he says to himself, Now that electronic communications are becoming global, anything is possible. How is he to know? Should he ask Ahmed if he is familiar with the articles? Bad idea. He might torture him even more cruelly.

Clenching his teeth, he decides not to say or do anything for the time being. He'll wait for the Italian.

In the course of the following night Shaltiel succeeded in persuading the Italian to remove his blindfold.

"In any case, it's of no use to you," he said. "I've studied esoteric subjects that have taught me how to 'see' voices. So I can describe you and your friend, your faces, your bodies, your behavior. Do you want me to prove it?"

The Italian nodded his head silently. He was surprised when his prisoner began to describe facial characteristics of both men—one bearded, the other just badly shaved; the first having well-defined eyebrows, the other bushy ones.

Luigi is thrown by what Shaltiel has to say, failing to account for the blindfold having been askew. He removes it. Shaltiel has won. He squints, adjusting his eyes to even the meager light.

Am I dreaming? Is it the dream that makes my body tremble? wonders Shaltiel. He is so afraid of torture, so afraid of fear. His brain is muddled, disoriented, especially when he must wear the blindfold. He keeps repeating prayers, but they are beginning to seem less holy. His thoughts are bizarre; he's not even sure he's *thinking*. Does he cry for help? The cry may well be silent. But he hears it and he's not sure it's him. He suddenly sees himself surrounded by a group of masked children who are threatening him. They're reproaching him for not having children. They demand a story, any story, as long as it's beautiful. He suggests a poem; they refuse. He insists. They put their hands over their ears. He gets angry. A little girl makes a face at him. He finds it unbearable. Finally, he submits:

This is the story of a young, sad tiger who, from afar, tells a beautiful story to an exhausted old lion. Listen, children, grandchildren, listen and don't cry. And you, old people, listen and don't laugh.

Don't look for your father, says the tiger; he is gone. Don't call for your mother; she is hiding.

What do you say, children, when you're saying nothing? And you, old people, what are you doing against the forest with its bruised arms?

And you, jailer, who is the real prisoner, you who erects great walls or me, your victim who dreams of freedom?

Let's listen, children, nice children, let's listen to the beggar who keeps silent and the blind man who sings of dusk and the tramp who sings of his thirst.

An awkward movement awakens him with a start.

.   .   .

To escape from the present, Shaltiel takes refuge in the delirium of the past: his father so pure in his occupations; his friends so compassionate; One-Eyed Paritus and his secrets; his brother, Pavel, and his metamorphoses; Blanca and lost happiness, un-fulfilled love.

I feel an obscure desire to compare my imprisonment and my abductors' death threats to the sufferings of my father, my mother and their parents. But I fight against the comparison. I confine myself to just recalling those years. Even in my imagination, I didn't accompany them far enough into the darkness. I learned from my father never to yield to the temptation of comparing. Some memories are by essence unique and must remain so: Any resemblance can only be illusory.

How, in their flesh and conscience, did he and his companions live through the German occupation and its atrocities? How did they live with the dead and with death all around them? They may talk about it if they have the strength and desire; others have done so. As for me, I won't allow myself to: I have no firsthand knowledge of Auschwitz and Ravensbrück. And there, the mystics are right: Those who know don't talk and those who talk don't know. And even the survivors who have decided to bear witness confirm it in their way: They almost all say that their experience can't be related in words, and yet, as witnesses, they're morally compelled to resort to them. Their silence, except if it is ontologically integral to their deposition, would not help truth triumph. It would only open the road to oblivion and, as one survivor put it, enable the executioner to kill his victims a second time.

To tell this story in its entirety, it may be useful for me to emphasize the role that the game of chess played in my life.

I like playing chess. I like the concentration it demands and the fact that imagination is essential. The notion that sometimes one needs to grant greater initiative and power to the pawn than the king. I welcome the need to anticipate the opponent's moves, and turn them against him.

I also like this intelligent game because it brings me closer to my father. Facing the chessboard, even when I'm alone, I'm never *really* alone—my father is always facing me. I like his generosity and his way of educating me, of loving me, and doing it without flaunting it. He does everything to give me confidence. At first he went to great lengths to lose against me. Later, he went to even greater lengths to win. And when he would lose, he was happy. And proud, very proud.

I would sometimes play with strangers, and more often still, alone. There was a time, at the age of twelve, as I was preparing for my bar mitzvah, when I preferred the game to studying. In fact, I had already acquired a reputation as a budding champion in Brooklyn.

My father also liked chess, though he sometimes chided me for playing too much. Seeing me without a book in my hands or under my arm, he would gently reprimand me: "Are you forgetting that losing a game is an error or a lesson, but losing one's time is a sin?" His rebukes never lasted very long. Afterward he watched me closely as I pondered the best way of exploiting the position of the mischievous pawn threatened by the horrid castle.

In Davarowsk, Galicia, several years earlier, I had the good fortune of meeting a German, Friedrich von Waldensohn, who claimed to be a count, though he didn't make his lineage clear. Austrian, Hungarian, Estonian, Prussian?

He lived in a large apartment near the Jewish neighborhood, but our first meeting took place at our house, well before we moved to the ghetto. One evening, he knocked at the door and announced he was looking for me. My father was gripped with fear: Was he with the police? What possibly could it be?

The visitor, noticing me at the other end of the room, made me come closer.

"He's young, barely seven," my father said. "He didn't do anything bad."

"I see all of you are frightened. Don't worry, I have no intention of harming you. I'm not a policeman. I'm here because I'm interested in chess; if I could, I'd spend my days and nights in front of the chessboard. And I'm told that you, my boy, are a good player."

I didn't know what to say. But my father quickly pulled himself together.

"Yes, that's true, my son is a good player—at least people say he is. But I'm not competent enough to judge."

"I am," said the visitor. And he turned to me. "What about you? What do you think?"

I don't know how I found the courage, if that's what it was, but I replied, "Would you like me to show you?"

In a split second the table was cleared and the chessboard appeared. The count and I, face-to-face, started a game whose repercussions would turn out to be considerable in all our lives. He spoke German and I, Yiddish.

I was nervous, anguished; I sensed danger. After all, I couldn't crawl into the man's head: Whether I won or lost, I risked sparking the anger of my distinguished opponent. I had to make an effort to concentrate. I had the luck of playing black. I had no trouble predicting his first four moves (the king's pawn, the queen's bishop . . .). I set up my attack. He repulsed it. After playing for over an hour, my eyes constantly on my fingers, I found myself at a turning point: Should I sacrifice my castle and then capture his queen three moves later and possibly humiliate him, and suffer his revenge? I wondered if he sensed I was hesitating. I sacrificed my castle—and I won the game. Stunned, frightened, my father stared at me, afraid that heaven would come tumbling down on us. But to our great surprise, my opponent, instead of being angry, showed contentment and approval.

"You almost kept the castle to keep me happy, right?"

I stammered some incoherent words. He interrupted me.

"Don't insult me by lying!" he snapped.

I didn't answer. But, as if at the edge of a precipice, I implored the God of my ancestors to protect us.

The visitor resumed in a friendlier voice.

"That was Alekhine's defense you used in the beginning, wasn't it?"

"I don't understand . . ."

"You're lying again! Do you think I don't know the gambits, the openings and defenses of the great Russian masters?"

My body in a sweat, all I could do was repeat, "Sir, you have to believe me . . ."

"My son never lies," my father interjected.

"I've never heard the word 'gambit,' " I said. "I've never heard that there were . . . there were masters, great or small."

The visitor scrutinized me for a long time, then gave me a faint smile.

"I believe you. And I like you. I'll take my revenge next week. Okay?"

"Of course, sir," my father replied, in my stead.

The war had been going on forever. Davarowsk was occupied by the Hungarian army and suffering under its yoke. Our Jewish community was soon to be subjected to the first anti-Semitic measures. Meanwhile, the number of disastrous decrees kept growing.

Friedrich von Waldensohn—or "the count" as we called him—came to see us every week. Our games were becoming more intense for both of us. They took place even in the ghetto, where we had moved with a few pitiful objects and utensils. Whenever he visited, he brought us food and sometimes much-needed clothes.

Usually, when we played, we hardly spoke about the political situation and the war, about which, in any case, I understood virtually nothing. The count alluded to them occasionally. "The world," he said one day, "is a huge chessboard. And we play for or against fate."

He was interested in everything that concerned me: my mother, who had become ill, my father's past and the education of my cousin Arele. Once, when we were alone, he dropped a remark, as he moved a pawn, that seemed innocuous.

"Apparently you have a brother, somewhere, who is older than your cousin."

I blushed. My heart began to beat very hard.

"Yes," I said.

"His name is . . . ?"

"Pinhas . . . Pavel."

"Where is he?"

"I don't know."

"Does your father know?"

"No."

"So, who does know?"

"No one."

He caressed his chin as though he were thinking about his next move. Then he played his knight and endangered my castle.

"We know where he is," he said

I almost asked, Who is "we"? but restrained myself. Given how much time we were spending together, I had stopped worrying about his origins. Going by his name, he was surely German.

"He's in Russia.

I bit my tongue.

"We know a lot of things about a lot of people," he continued.

A sudden rush of fear made me commit an error—I took a pawn and lost my castle. I saw everything in a blur. No game had ever required so much concentration from me; it was both painful and exciting.

He raised his head and looked at me.

"I can see I frightened you. Fear is a luxury to which chess players are not entitled."

Interrupting the game, he took advantage of the fact that

we were alone to confide in me: As a German, and thanks to his authentic aristocratic titles, he had been recruited by the intelligence services of the occupation authorities.

"As long as I'm here," he said, "you and your family have nothing to fear."

That evening, I told my father about this latest development. He was returning from work in the forest. My cousin hadn't yet returned from the clandestine school where he was in charge of a dozen children younger than he.

"I should have suspected it," said my father, his face clouding over. "How else could he go freely in and out of the ghetto? And now that we know, how can we trust him? In fact, now that I think about it, I'm worried by what he just told you. As long as he's here, probably we have nothing to fear. But that means that the other people here have everything to fear—that's what his comments mean. There's a new danger threatening our community. I'm afraid this foreshadows horrible events for the ghetto."

"Why do you see everything as so dire, Father? Yes, he's German, but he's not like the others!"

"You say that because he likes to play chess?"

"No, because he's never been cruel with us. He never takes advantage of the situation to humiliate us. And you have to admit he's always shown lots of consideration and even been generous with us."

"With us, yes," said my father, looking more and more worried. "But with the other Jews? What do we know about his attitude toward them? Maybe he's preparing to unleash even greater misfortunes on our people?"

My cousin Arele joined us then, bringing bad news.

"The Germans have learned of the existence of the schools

in the ghetto," he said. "They're outraged. A member of the Jewish Council reported it to us. A German officer yelled, 'What's going on here? It's unthinkable, intolerable, illegal and criminal! While German and Hungarian soldiers are fighting in Russia around the clock, gloriously serving the Nazi ideal, some little Jews are sitting here quietly studying the Bible as if nothing were happening!' I'm afraid our schools are going to be banned."

My father looked at me. I had seldom seen him look so troubled.

For one or two weeks, the count, even-tempered, came back for our chess games. As usual, he brought bread and sometimes even butter or plum jam. In principle we were equal opponents before the chessboard. He found my game increasingly daring; his was inspired. We always learned a great deal from each other.

"When I was thirteen," he remarked one day, "I was as good as you are. And then I lost my father. He was killed in action. For a whole year, I couldn't look at a chessboard. The image of his mutilated body haunted all my thoughts. I swore I would take revenge."

I felt my opponent was becoming increasingly preoccupied, perturbed, melancholic. Could my father be right? Was the count a harbinger of turmoil and renewed harassments?

Now, in the place where I am, between these four filthy walls, a toy in the hands of my torturers, I discovered that in life, though man doesn't know it, he sometimes plays with or opposite Death. Is the choice in our hands?

Yes, my father had been right in his apprehensions.

That afternoon we had expected Friedrich von Waldensohn at the usual hour, but he had not arrived. While we waited for him in our little room, Father boiled water and Arele studied the Midrash of the Psalms. I was in front of the chessboard trying to work my way through the game that had been left unfinished at our last meeting. At twilight, the count walked in without knocking, empty-handed. He didn't take his place at the table, as was his habit, but remained standing and addressed my father.

"Time is short. You're going to leave this place and the ghetto. I've prepared a secure shelter for you. Take as few things as possible. Hurry up."

He looked at me and said, "We'll finish our game some other time. Right now we're playing against a common opponent, and he's powerful."

A common opponent? I wondered if he was referencing a previous conversation when he had talked about destiny and death to my father. What if the two were the same?

While my father looked around deciding which things to take, he asked the count what would happen to my mother: Her intestinal disorder had become worse, the pain unbearable, and the physicians had planned on surgery. "Don't be afraid; we're not going to prevent her being operated on! We Germans aren't savages, sir!"

And what was going to happen to the other Jews in the ghetto, our cousins and nephews and nieces, among others? Could we help them too? The count answered in a firm, steady voice.

"Only one part of the ghetto will be evacuated at dawn.

Unfortunately I can't do anything for the other members of your family. I don't have space for that many people. And eventually it would get around. You have to admit, the risk is too great, for you and for me."

"But where will they be taken?" my father asked. "And for how long?"

"I repeat: Time is short. Don't keep asking me questions that I can't answer."

"And what about my mother? Are you sure she'll stay here?"

"And that we'll see her again soon?" my cousin added.

"There are some good surgeons in the ghetto. After all, don't they say that Jewish doctors are the best?"

The count was lying shamelessly. The Jewish hospital was about to be cleared of its occupants. And the patients, even my poor mother, even those unfit to be moved, were dragged into military trucks and driven to the freight station, among the first deported.

But we didn't yet know this.

Night was falling. The sky had become gray and clouded, and a fine, slow rain streamed down as we left the ghetto, like shadows, preceded by the count.

We were saved.

We were the only survivors.

My mother, Miriam, with her smile, her lullabies. My uncle Leib, a furrier; his wife, Tsirele, and their three children; my cousins Itzikl, Shloimele and Sorele; my aunt Revtsu, a sickly widow; my friends Oïzer'l, Shmulik, Naftoli and Hayimi— their laughter, their singing, the movements of their hands as they delved into an ancient text, their warm gestures when they shared a piece of fruit with me . . .

Evacuated, all of them, in leaden freight cars. Gone. Forever.

Is it true that the count couldn't have saved them? Or didn't he want to?

Were they doomed because they didn't know how to play chess or because I played too well?

The count housed us in the basement of a building next to his, which he owned. No one would have dared to enter without permission, or without being accompanied by the owner or his servant, Dorothea. She was an elderly woman, dark-haired and dark-eyed, silent. She had been his governess and later his secretary, carrying out the duties of a chambermaid as well. He trusted her and so did we. She took care of us as if we were members of the count's family.

Once or twice a week, in the evening, he came downstairs to check that everything was in order. Then he would bring me to his house and into his study, where we would play our chess games that sometimes lasted for several sittings. Sometimes he won. Often I let myself be beaten because, in spite of his warnings, something told me that it was better not to have too many victories.

And life continued.

Today, in my subterranean imprisonment, plunged in dark patches of eternity, I can only evoke my parents' life in the past. As a child I already lived in my imagination on occasion: I "saw" blossoming trees or trees laden with snow; I "smelled" the odor of a horse; I "heard" the meowing of a cat; I "tasted" the butter or honey on the table; I "watched" with an almost happy feeling as the crimson clouds gently disappeared in a reddening sky.

Did I think of God too, of His presence in history? Before the ghetto and during my parents' first days there, I'm certain that they always led a Jewish life, conforming to the rules and customs of our religion. So did I. They observed the Sabbath and fasted on the designated fasting days. (I didn't fast because I was still too young.) Later, in the hideaway where the count had moved us, this way of life became impossible. How can wine be blessed if there's no wine? How can the Lord be thanked for His kindness, His mercy, His enlightenment when we were suffocating in a dark basement?

My father, Arele, I—we all had to be cautious. My German protector—I'll come back to this later—said this to me repeatedly, as he looked down on the chessboard, lit by candlelight.

He said: "Without me you and your family would have been lost. That's why I have to be extra vigilant too."

Sometimes, when German officers visited their comrade, my father and I were afraid of breathing too noisily.

On the anniversary of my grandmother's deportation—dressed like a peasant woman, she had thought she could get bread from the priest in the neighboring village, but was caught in a roundup—my father couldn't hold back his tears.

"It isn't even possible to recite the Kaddish here in her memory."

He was seriously considering a brief return to the ghetto. "It's easier to find a minyan there."

After Arele talked him out of it, he said, "These days I say to myself that perhaps the Lord was more charitable toward her by taking her away from us. She would not have lived through our misfortunes."

From time to time, our benefactor informed us of what was happening inside the ghetto. Hunger, overcrowding, disappearances.

"Though I don't believe in God," he used to say, "a useless invention of the Jews, and in the end an evil one, I'm grateful to Him for not being born Jewish."

Later, my father said to me, "As for me, I'm grateful to the Lord for not being born German."

"As for me," said Arele, "I'm just sorry I was born."

The following week, our benefactor told us, not without pride, how he had saved a Jewish adolescent.

"A member of the SS caught him yesterday evening near the barbed wire: Either he wanted to sneak out to get to the Aryan side or he was sneaking back in. Naturally, the soldier gave him a thrashing and the authorities sentenced him to death. The public execution was scheduled for this morning. But when I saw the adolescent's wounds, I don't know why, I suddenly felt a kind of pity for him, something I usually don't feel. I lied to the SS commander. 'This young Jew,' I said to him, 'surely belongs to a resistance movement. So I must question him. It's part of my responsibilities. Once I've pried his secrets from him, I'll hand him over to you.' It was an argument that even an SS commander can't refute. Therefore, thanks to me, your chess opponent, a young Jew, is still alive."

"Alive for how long?"

"For a few hours, a few days."

"And then?"

"Then he won't suffer anymore."

"Did you question him yet?"

"Not yet. I told the SS that he was too badly beaten and not in good enough condition to undergo our questioning."

"And when he's in a proper condition, then what?"

"Right now, he's alive, whereas he could have died this morning," replied the count, looking annoyed. "Be happy with that."

My father, who was near me, intervened. "If the questioning lasts long enough, can't we hope for a miracle?"

Friedrich von Waldensohn didn't bother to answer.

The boy was hanged two days later. The count announced this to us while thinking about how to avoid a trap set by my bishop. He won the game.

One evening, my opponent arrived in a friendly mood, sat down on a stool and asked me to put the chessboard away.

"Not tonight. My head is elsewhere. I have bad news. The last Jews are going to be evacuated. The ghetto will be liquidated."

"Do they know?" asked my father, downcast.

"No, they don't."

"Why not warn some of them? They might be able to escape and save their lives. There are so few left."

"Perfectly useless," said the count. "First of all, the ghetto is surrounded by SS and by the local fascists. It's sealed. Secondly, because of my duties, I belong to a restricted circle of people who know the details of this kind of operation. If a single Jew is captured and says he knew of the upcoming liquidation, I would be in danger of being compromised. The investigation could lead to me. And then, what about your fate? Has that occurred to you? For my fellow officers, this is not a chess game; for them, the Jewish problem is not a game. It excites their passions. They won't know the joy of victory, even temporarily, as long as there is a single Jew alive somewhere."

Nonetheless, shortly after the count left, Arele and my father went to the ghetto, first to warn the few friends who were still living there about the looming danger, and then, foolishly, in order to recite the Kaddish. Even young as I was, I tried in vain to dissuade them. In vain. My father was convinced that, knowing the area better than the enemy, he and Arele could make a quick round-trip successfully.

It was reckless and absurd on their part. At four in the morning they still had not returned. I felt like screaming with despair. How could I contact the count? He alone could save my father and my cousin.

He obviously knew about their initiative, for he came to see me very early in the morning and was furious, ready to punch me with his two lumberjack's fists.

"What got into them? How could they ignore my warnings? Why did your father put his life in danger? Was it a fit of insanity?"

I didn't bother explaining to him that my father couldn't help wanting to come to the aid of the ghetto. And that he wanted to recite the Kaddish there.

A crazy thought went through my mind: Why didn't I offer to play a game of chess with the count, stipulating that if I won, he would bring back my father and cousin. It *was* crazy, but I summoned the courage to ask the question.

The count's face hardened; then he agreed.

How can one entrust wooden pieces with the life and death of loved ones? A doubt crawled into my mind and it upset my concentration: Even if I won, wouldn't the count go back on his promise brutally and with impunity?

The question was beside the point. I lost. The count was kind enough to comfort me instead of telling me the blunt truth.

"First of all," he said, "the deported are not going very far; they'll be back. Secondly, even if you had won, it wouldn't have changed anything. It's too late to step in and do anything. The ghetto is already being emptied. The freight cars are filling up."

My father and Arele returned—after the war. Their empty eyes stared into space then, and they had numbers tattooed on their arms.

Dorothea, the count's governess, how old could she have been? I was too young to care. In fact, for a long time I remained convinced that women were primarily for others.

Then Blanca chose me. It is a fact. Undeniable. Though she didn't succeed in changing my life, she did change many things in my life. Even if it had been a long time since I expected love to bring happiness. I don't feel like struggling to justify love anymore. But I admit that, thanks to Blanca, I've succeeded in getting closer to my truth. Or in simpler terms: After about twenty years, I was finally able answer a question that had troubled me for a long time. Was Blanca really the only woman in my life?

Until the end of the occupation, I lived in the officially "empty" and dilapidated house of Count Friedrich von Waldensohn. Even though he was protecting me, I lived in anguish.

With time, I wanted to believe that in spite of my Jewish origins, the German count liked me. Didn't he pluck me out of the ranks because he discovered me in front of a chessboard? Was it that he appreciated my way of playing? What intrigued him most, I think, was my natural talent, a hereditary gift no doubt (was one of my ancestors a grand master?). As a boy, I owed nothing to the handbooks and their teachings, all based on the methods of the illustrious champions whose names I didn't even know. I had told the count: I had never heard of Alekhine's valiant gambit or Steinberg's original defense. In fact, I didn't need examples. I followed my intuition.

I missed my family, of course. Sometimes, when I was lonely, I couldn't prevent tears from streaming down my face. Sometimes I would cry silently even while I was considering my strategy as we played. The count would try to calm and console me.

"Your loved ones aren't far away, I guarantee it. They're working, like everyone, but they're well."

Could I believe him? I tried to convince myself that he was my protector, that he cared about me. Why would he lie? But deep down, I mistrusted him, though of course I never showed it for fear of arousing his anger.

The count was such a good liar. One day, with my heart in my mouth, I asked him, "You say my family is well and not far from here. But what about my mother? How is she? She has intestinal problems. She was going to be operated on."

"Oh yes, she was very sick. But she recovered. I'm positive; I got it straight from her physician. The one who operated on her. In fact, if you want, you could write her a little note; I'll give it to her when I next visit her camp."

Naturally, I quickly composed a letter, expressing in Yiddish all my nostalgia, sorrow, loneliness and love. The count tried to read it but gave up; he remarked that he didn't know my language, which seemed to him a vulgar corruption of German, but that he trusted me. My note would be given to her within a week.

One week later, he was beaming.

"Mission accomplished. Your mother cried when she read your letter. She showed it to everyone. It was a good idea you had, a generous idea, my boy. Now that contact has been established, things will go better."

He was such a good liar. Was it because everything was like chess to him? Aren't we liars or actors, to a lesser or greater extent, when we play chess? Tricking the opponent's vigilance, isn't that a lie?

In my subterranean hideaway, I was worried. As I had no contact with the world outside, I was ignorant of what was happening to the Jews under the enemy's yoke.

My father, I learned later, suffered through illness and despair in Auschwitz. Most of his relatives and friends had died long before; in fact, some of them, including my grandmother, died the very night they arrived in Birkenau.

Miraculously, Arele and my father survived. To the bitter end of the war, they worked together in Auschwitz, providing support for each other.

As the weeks and months went by in the summer of 1944, everyone understood that the evacuation of the ghetto meant that the war, and therefore the occupation, the apotheosis of evil, was coming to an end. The count knew full well that the Red Army was approaching Kolomea; often, in the evening, we could hear the artillery in the distance.

The count was preoccupied about what would happen

"afterward." What would he do when the retreat order was given? he asked himself out loud. Would he be transferred to the front, to the rear? For how long?

And I had anxious thoughts too: If he leaves, what will become of me?

One evening, he came down the stairs to the hideaway, where I was reading by candlelight. I assumed he wanted to play chess and I started to put out the board.

"No," he said. "No need to anymore. It's over. I have to leave the city. I wouldn't like to fall into the hands of the Russians."

He paused for a moment before continuing.

"The city is almost entirely surrounded. The battle won't last long. Our defenses are too weak and we're going to set up a well-organized retreat. I think that the day after tomorrow, you'll be able to go upstairs. Dorothea is staying here. She'll take care of you. But . . ."

Another pause.

"No doubt you'll be questioned about me. Remember the fact that you're still alive and more or less free. You owe it to me."

I thought to myself: No, he's wrong. That's not true. I owe the fact that I'm still alive to his and my passion for an ancient, constantly reinvented game. Fearful as I was, I kept silent. Why annoy the count by contradicting him? As long as he was still around, he was dangerous, all-powerful.

He smiled ambiguously, melancholically or pusillanimously—I couldn't tell—and shook my hand before leaving.

.   .   .

A few hours later, the Red Army's heavy artillery shelled Dava-rowsk. As a result, I was no longer the only person to breathe the underground dust. All of the city's inhabitants congregated in the antiaircraft shelters. There was not a single Jew among them. They had all been swept into a tempest of fire and hatred. The sensation was strange: I was the only young descendant of Abraham, Isaac and Jacob, the last disciple of Moses and Rabbi Akiba, in a dark, condemned world, about to reawaken on the ruins of its memory and hope.

Contrary to what the count had said, Dorothea was nowhere to be seen. Had she followed her master? Returned to Germany perhaps? Or had she taken refuge at the house of relatives, or civilians, far from the front? Was she afraid of the inevitable reprisals of the population who had had to serve the Germans for so long? Other pro-Nazi collaborators had fled for the same reason. It was predictable, crystal clear: The hour of the dispensers of justice and avengers had finally arrived.

How many more days and nights was I going to stay all alone, without help and without food, in this hideaway where fear was my only faithful companion?

I tried to pass the time by resuming a game I had started with the count. But my brain wasn't working very well any-more. More and more anguished, I couldn't concentrate. The black and white pieces seemed perturbed and disoriented on the chessboard, reflecting my mood. The pieces seemed to move of their own free will following an ever-changing strategy. Indif-ferent to propriety, the bishop laughed, the knight danced, the queen cried and the king, motionless and impassive, bit his lips as he waited for the near and distant future.

The count had seen things accurately. The nightmare ended two days after his departure.

Noisily busting the door open, an electric flashlight in one hand, a cocked machine gun in the other, a bearded giant, as big as a mountain bear, stepped in slowly and cautiously. He wore a padded winter jacket and a fur hat. On the hat was a five-pointed star. Suddenly he jumped near me and cried out orders in Russian, which I understood thanks to my Slavic acquaintances.

"Are there any Germans here? Answer quickly."

"No," I answered, "I'm all alone."

"Are you sure?"

"Yes. I'm all alone."

He searched the shadowy corners with his flashlight and settled on my frightened face.

"You're shaking with fear. What or who are you afraid of now that the Germans are gone? Don't you see I'm your liberator?"

"Yes, I do."

He noticed the chessboard.

"You play chess?"

"Yes."

"With who?"

"All alone."

He examined the positions and said, "The black knight is clever. If I had time, I'd prove it to you, but the Red Army has other things in store for me. We're on our way to Berlin. Hitler is kaput, even if his stupid soldiers don't know it yet."

I smiled faintly.

"You're Jewish?" the Russian soldier asked.

"Yes."

"That's why you're hiding?"

"Yes."

"And what about your family? Where are they?"

"I don't know. They've all left me."

He handed me a piece of bread. "I'm Jewish too. My name is Piotr. What's yours?"

"Shalti."

"My Jewish name is Peretz. What's yours?"

"Shaltiel."

"Okay, my friend Shalti. You're alive—that's all that counts. Do you hear the shooting? They're fighting in the nearby streets. Every building is being searched. They've already caught a German solider in civilian dress. No doubt there are others. It will all be over by tonight or tomorrow morning. You'll be able to go home. I have to leave you now. But I'll be back. I promise. But . . ." He cut himself short, surprised by his own ignorance. "Where's home?"

I burst out crying. "I don't know. I don't know anymore. I'm waiting for them, all of them. My parents . . . I don't know where they are now or what happened to them. But I'm waiting for them."

The soldier put down his flashlight and patted me on the shoulder. "Okay, my little Jewish brother. I understand you. You don't want to go back to an empty house. So wait here, upstairs. Do you want to?"

"Yes, I do."

"Then good-bye, Shaltiel."

"Good-bye, Peretz."

He hesitated a minute, then added, "Be careful, my friend.

When I'm with others, it's best to forget my Jewish name. Call me Piotr."

He left, and I started sobbing again.

Upstairs, I found the governess straightening up the place. Miraculously, the building had remained intact. I was more surprised than she. Without a word, she handed me a bowl of warm tea. I asked her if she had any news from the count. She hesitated before answering. I felt that my question made her ill at ease and irritated her.

"No news. He left with the army and won't be back. What about you? What are you going to do? Where are you going to live? Who will take care of you?"

I had never seen her so talkative.

"I think I'll be going home soon," I said. "But not right away. I'm waiting for someone who promised he'd come back to see me."

"Who's that?"

"His name is Piotr."

Her eyes fluttered nervously, and she shuddered when she heard the name. I wondered what she was so frightened of?

"Who is he?" she whispered in a hoarse voice.

"A soldier."

"A soldier!" she cried out, her hand over her mouth.

"A Russian officer." And after a pause. "He's Jewish . . . like me."

Panic-stricken, she left me brusquely and went into the kitchen.

. . .

Piotr reappeared two days later. I was waiting for him in the street. He brought me shirts and winter clothes, food and coal.

"Gifts from German citizens," he said, laughing noisily. "They led the good life here. Now it's your turn."

The governess wasn't at home.

Piotr helped me settle into the living room, which I wasn't familiar with. He left me a piece of paper with his address in Kiev for after the war.

"That way, you'll have someone to look up when you're over there."

I told him we already had someone over there. "My older brother. A Communist to the bone."

Seeing his stupefaction, I told him the story of my brother, a devoted admirer of Stalin, who had left the family and gone to the Soviet Union.

"And where is he?"

"I have no idea. He may have joined a relative of ours who lives in Moscow, apparently. At home, they used to say that he worked for a very important person."

"What's his name?"

"Leon. Leon Meirovitch."

"What! Repeat what you just said."

"Leon Meirovitch."

"You're pulling my leg, Shalti?"

"Of course not. Why would I?"

The soldier rose from his seat and started clapping his hands excitedly. "The great, illustrious, one and only Leon Meirovitch is his brother's boss, a member of his family, and he tells me this as though he were your ordinary corner grocer!"

He sat down again and took my hands. "Listen closely, child. I have to leave for the front again. I'll do my best to return. I want to make sure I can find you again."

"But I don't think I'll be living here."

"Where would you live?"

"Home. I'll wait for my relatives to return. Some of them may have died, but not all of them. At least, that's what I hope."

Piotr thought for a moment, then tore a sheet out of his notebook (which he had taken from a German). "Give me your old address."

I wrote it down and handed it to him.

We embraced. As I watched him leave, I wondered: Who will I see first, him or my family? To whom will I tell the story of how I survived?

A few days later, I "moved home," as they say, with a bundle of belongings packed by the governess. Except it wasn't our home anymore. A family of strangers had moved in, an emaciated, surly man, a sad-looking woman and two unruly children. I told them who I was, and they looked at me uncomprehendingly at first, then with hostility.

"Go away!" yelled the man. "We live here; it's our house. Go back to where you came from. Otherwise . . ."

He took out of his pocket a certifying document with official stamps.

Why argue with him? As he was on the verge of pushing me out the door, I left and went to the police. An indifferent police chief explained to me that hundreds of apartments and houses vacated during the occupation by their Jewish residents had been assigned to the homeless people from the neighboring cities and towns who had been bombed out and lost everything they owned. "We had to put them up somewhere, didn't we?"

I asked him where I should go. He shrugged his shoulders. I wanted to explain to him that if I didn't live at home, my parents, when they returned, wouldn't know where to find me.

He snickered. "There must be orphanages for kids like you."

"But I'm not an orphan! My parents are going to return!"

He dismissed me with an impatient gesture.

Back in the street, under a blazing sun, I couldn't hold back my tears. I walked aimlessly, for how long I don't know, until I was stopped by a Russian soldier who was coming out of a commandeered building. He asked me why I was crying. I told him that I didn't know where to go, that I no longer had a place to live, and especially that I was afraid of being permanently separated from my family. The Germans had taken them away . . .

"What's your name?" the soldier asked me.

I told him.

"Are you Jewish?"

"Yes."

Another stroke of luck: The man I stood in front of, Mendel, was Jewish.

"Come with me," he said.

Everything happened very quickly. The police chief had to apologize to me; he almost had to get on his knees. Then he walked us back to my house. The tall, skinny man who had chased me away was told that the house, as well as the furniture and the objects, had to be returned to me, and thoroughly cleaned and spotless from top to bottom, within twenty-four hours.

"But the official document," the man stammered.

The policeman looked at the Russian soldier, took the document, tore it up and threw it on the ground.

"We'll be back tomorrow morning," said the soldier. "If we find you here, you'll be sorry. You don't mess with the Red Army, you filthy anti-Semites!"

I thought of my Communist brother who had been gone for so long: If all the Soviets were like these soldiers, I could understand his passion for world revolution.

How was I to adapt to this new life?

This war wasn't like the others. In the past, death struck down adults at the front, but children and old people were protected. In this war, that wasn't true.

Little by little, the survivors started returning to Davarowsk. Most of them were young people. There were no children or old people. A small community was forming to help the lost and the needy. A rabbi officiated at a study and prayer house, and I went there. Like my father, I liked to pray with others.

It was there in that shrine, weeks after the Germans had left, that one Sabbath day a miracle befell me. As tradition required, the rabbi was reading the weekly passage of the Torah, when the door opened. My father and Arele appeared. I rushed to them, breathless. And all the faithful turned to look at us, as well as the rabbi, who quickly interrupted his reading.

Three Jews embraced one another as they wept.

My father and Arele were returning from the kingdom of

darkness where humanity had been brought down, crushed, almost annihilated beyond recall.

Auschwitz.

I asked about Mama.

They shook their heads.

She had been trampled on, wounded, humiliated, suffocated and burned on the very night of her arrival. A member of the Sonderkommandos had confirmed it.

My opponent, the count, that bastard, I thought. My German protector had lied to me, misled me, betrayed me. How could I forgive that?

We spent days and nights holding hands in our house, looking tenderly at one another, exchanging our recollections and experiences with inadequate words, and our silences, especially our silences—there were some things we couldn't say.

One day when we were talking about the war, Father said, "I survived thanks to Arele. He was my support."

"And you, mine," said Arele.

"I survived thanks to chess," I said, "and a German officer." My father nodded.

"Where is he? What became of him?" Arele asked.

"I was hoping to see him again and tell him what I think of him. I have a score to settle, questions to ask. He should be tried and sentenced, punished. He was an officer of the Sicherheitsdienst, it turns out, not without influence. He could have prevented the hanging of the Jewish boy, Mama's deportation and yours. He made a fool of me, of all of us. The only thing that interested him in life was chess. The power to defeat his opponent, to win. Human lives didn't count for him. He trampled us Jews as if we were scum."

"I wonder where Pinhas is," my father said.

"It was such a long time ago. We were so miserable when he left, but he did well to leave."

"Maybe we'll know one day," I said, thinking of the first Jewish Red Army soldier who rescued me at that tragic moment in my life.

"How?"

A spark of joy lit up inside me. It chased away shadows and ghosts and revealed a brother, an older brother in full force.

I told them about my meeting with Piotr.

"He wanted to know everything about me. It seems that Pavel is a very important person over there. He works for . . ."

"Leon Meirovitch? Our relative?" my father asked.

"Yes. In fact, Piotr promised to come back to see me. I gave him our address."

"Who knows what happened to him?" Arele wondered. "The war isn't over yet. Everything is still chaotic."

"He'll keep his promise," I said in an obstinate tone of voice.

Given history's convulsions, we had every reason not to hold out much hope. Yet my father remarked, "And the fact that we're here—true, not all of us, but some of us—in our own house, among ourselves, reunited, and the fact that there are still Jews in Europe, isn't that the sign that miracles can still happen?"

His face darkened suddenly as he no doubt thought of his wife and others who suffered a similar fate. The word "miracle" resonated like a kind of blasphemy.

. . .

Shaltiel summoned memories and faces as a way of protecting himself, shielding himself from the torturers. His moments of complete dejection, the feeling of plummeting into bottomless depths, was thereby mitigated by the glimmers of ecstasy. He shivered with cold, yet was bathed in sweat.

Outside, life triumphs. There are cries and tears of victory, fascism defeated, Nazism humiliated. The horror of the German dictatorship is unmasked. Suffering the worst defeat in its history, Germany has lost all its pride. Europe is liberated. The Jewish people have survived. Shouts of "Hurrah" are heard in Moscow and Kiev. People dance in the streets of Paris and Amsterdam. There are military parades everywhere. The Resistance is jubilant. "Never again" becomes more than a slogan: It's a prayer, a promise, a vow. There will never again be hatred, people say. Never again jail and torture. Never again the suffering of innocent people, or the shooting of starving, frightened, terrified children. And never again the glorification of base, ugly, dark violence. It's a prayer.

One autumn day, my father is rereading letters sent to friends in Palestine and America: requests for advice and help. It is our joint decision to leave Europe. It feels urgent to escape from the land and the clouds that witnessed the death of so many of our people, abandoned by God and betrayed by His creation. We want to start a new family life elsewhere, far from the cemeteries embedded in our recollections of ashes and blazing skies.

Arele is engrossed in a history book.

I'm still clinging to the chessboard.

Someone knocks at the door.

"Go see who's there," says my father.

When I see who it is, I shout so loudly that it could wake a deaf person on the other side of the ocean. "Piotr!"

I fall into his strong arms. He laughs; his whole body is laughing.

He shouts in a strong, booming voice, "So, little man, you thought I had forgotten you, huh?"

My father and Arele are standing behind me, waiting for the reunion scene to end. I introduce them to Piotr. He removes his rucksack and opens it. It contains coffee, sugar, flour, chocolate, condensed milk—all American products, the riches of our pitiable world. He hands them to my father, who is so overcome with emotion that he doesn't take them right away.

"Before anything," he says, "I have to shake your hand. My son told me so much about you that I feel I've known you since the beginning of my life."

Returning home from Berlin, Piotr stays with us for several days. We each talk about our war experiences. "I know Auschwitz," says Piotr, looking fixedly at my father and cousin. He wants to see their tattooed numbers. He shuts his eyes and opens them, shaking his head incredulously. Some of his comrades liberated Birkenau and other extermination camps. Their thirst for revenge was not to be believed.

"Whatever sufferings we now impose on the Germans," he said, "they deserve. They deserve much worse. They're living in fear and, let's hope, haunted by remorse and shame. Russian soldiers frighten them, and when the Russian soldier happens to be Jewish, their fear is a thousand times more intense. They see me as a pure avenger, thirsting for their blood. Yet, God is my witness, I didn't touch a single woman. Seeing them grovel before me is enough. But tell me, Shaltiel, who's living in the house where I met you?"

"I don't know. I never set foot there again."

"Why don't we go?"

"What for?" my father asks.

"Simple curiosity. Since it used to belong to a German officer, probably a Soviet officer lives there now."

"Fine. Let's go there."

"All of us?"

"Why not?" says my father.

We go there on foot. As we walk, Piotr describes the street fighting in Berlin, one building at a time, and the fanatical Hitler Youth who defended the privileged neighborhoods near the Chancellery. He asks me: "What became of your German?"

"I have no idea. Maybe he's dead. Maybe he's in Berlin."

"Maybe I killed him," says Piotr.

We laugh while we walk on. A shiver runs down my spine when we've arrived. It's the end of the afternoon. In the coolness of dusk a little wind is blowing in from the mountains. It brought to mind nights tormented by nightmares. Memories of chess games brought anguish. I recalled the fear of winning and the fear of losing: How was I to guess the mood and thoughts of my opponent, my enemy? I remembered waiting for the following day and its uncertainties, and the loneliness, as I brooded over my father. It all came to the surface and swirled around in my memory.

Here we are in front of the house. I had expected to come

upon ruins, but it hadn't changed. The tree was still there in the garden, carrying yellow leaves. I could sometimes see them from below, in the hideaway. I wished I could touch them, confide in them.

There is light in the windows. I knock on the door lightly. After a moment, it opens. An elderly, stooped woman appears and with a clumsy movement quickly tries to shut the door; the sight of the Russian officer has frightened her. Piotr prevents it. She sees us behind him. In spite of the darkness, I see panic etched on Dorothea's face.

"We'd like to go inside," says Piotr in Yiddish.

She doesn't move. He eases her gently out of the way. Her gaze has not left me. I can read her thoughts, her astonishment, her feelings of helplessness, as though she were facing a great danger: "You . . . you . . . what do you want? What are you doing here?"

Suddenly, it becomes clear that she is hiding someone. I point to the secret door leading to the underground hideaway. She almost collapses, stifling a cry.

There he was. The count. He was hiding there in the very place where I had hid, where I had found asylum against crushing misery. He is pale, as I had most likely been several months before, thinner too. He is still dressed elegantly: a white shirt and a black tie.

He is sitting wide-eyed, at "my" table, in front of a chessboard, maybe ours. I wondered whose presence frightens him more, mine or the Russian officer's.

"That's him?" Piotr asks.

"Yes. Count Friedrich von Waldensohn, officer of the SD, in person," says my father.

Piotr asks him a few questions in Russian, which I translate. He doesn't answer. Piotr becomes incensed.

"He better open his mouth or I'll take him straight to the Kommandantur! There he'll be taught respect."

We are speaking Yiddish, but the count gleans the meaning of the words. He stands up, bows and states his rank. He says I can vouch for his innocence: He has never tortured anyone, killed anyone or arrested anyone. He held only a desk job, he says, far from the scene of action. He merely studied and evaluated the information provided by his subordinates, and later passed it on to his superiors.

"Is this true?" Piotr asks me.

"Yes and no."

"Explain, please."

"I never saw him kill anyone, but he lied to me about my mother, my father and my cousin. My mother was already dead and burned, and my father and cousin deported to Auschwitz when he claimed he had run into them in a camp not far from here."

"Translate," the count demands of me.

I do, and he shrugs his shoulders.

"I had no choice," he says. "I had to lie to you. The truth would have driven you to despair. Also, you wouldn't have been able to concentrate on your game."

"Yes," I say bitterly. "I used to play chess with him. In order to survive. I had to."

My father, Arele and Piotr seem stunned. They can't understand. While they were suffering in the throes of hell, I was playing chess with a German officer who was more concerned about my powers of concentration than the fate of my loved ones? Piotr asks him to sit down, while we remain standing. Dorothea nervously says she is sorry she can't offer us anything, not even tea.

Piotr stares at her with a look of disgust.

"His Lordship isn't guilty," she says. "He must not be taken to jail. He merely did his duty. He never hurt anyone."

Piotr motions to her to stop talking. She retires to a corner of the basement, buries her head in her hands and sobs convulsively.

"I'm taking him in," Piotr says to me. "I have to deliver him to the Soviet military authorities. His fate doesn't depend on me. Maybe on you."

"I don't understand."

"Since you know him, you'll have to testify."

The count cuts in. "You'll testify on my behalf, won't you? You'll tell them I treated you well, that I protected you, that I took a big risk keeping you with me?"

He spoke Russian after all. A thorough man of deceit.

The count stares at me with his cold, penetrating gaze. "Shaltiel, do you remember what I said to you when we separated? I told you to remember that you owed me your life, do you remember?"

"Yes, I remember. And I replied that I owed my life to chess."

"But you played with me!"

"No. Not with you, with Death."

Piotr remains pondering. Then he grabs the count. He will deliver him to headquarters. It is his duty as an officer.

At that very moment, I decide never again to look at a chessboard. But with the passing of time, I couldn't keep my promise.

From all quarters, he is being asked to talk about it. What was it like? His first sensations. The turning points. When did he feel his suffering was intolerable? And was death to be desired or inevitable? And the possibility, if not the certainty, of being rescued, when did that feeling come? And being liberated, what was that like?

He shakes his head: No, not yet. Another time. Later. Oh, he's well aware of what he owes them. If he's still alive, if he's breathing, if he feels able to resume his life, to renew relationships and even deepen them—he will repay his debt to them. But he can't now fulfill the questioners' expectations. Or satisfy those of the journalists. Everything in its own time. One day, he'll talk. He'll find the words. He'll write.

He'll also talk about the one who is missing.

Of the two torturers, which one is more dangerous? Luigi with his provocative, intelligent remarks, or Ahmed with his temper tantrums? The former, calm, unflappable, ghostly, tries to appeal to one's humanity; the latter, on the contrary, fiery and on edge, plays at making one feel useless, weak and scorned.

Through an opening somewhere—the small basement window or a door left ajar to let some air in—comes the noise from outside: the racket of garbage collectors, kids playing, adults running, the complaints of some, the laughter of others, birds chirping. Yes, there are still free human beings who exercise their freedom and humanity for good or ill.

The hostage keeps his swollen eyes open. Time flows, but its rhythm changes radically. Therein lies the tragedy: In order to break with the present, from which there is no present means of escape, he tries to recapture the recent or distant past, elusive as it is, moving within a personal time frame that sometimes heeds him, sometimes slips away from him. Time drags on, then suddenly, for no apparent reason, speeds forward, rushing with an implacable yet hidden logic.

The hostage invents his own clock, his own measuring system. He recites the first chapter of the Psalms; that must take a minute. For the fifth, he needs four. The biblical story of the *Akedah,* or the near sacrifice of Isaac: three minutes. The commentaries: an hour and a half. *Antigone:* eighty minutes. A hundred for Aesop's fables. A few of Satan's monologues in Milton's *Paradise Lost:* thirty-two.

What does Maimonides say about the legal problem of hostages? What is the duty of the community when it comes to paying a ransom?

His brain is working, his memory too; Shaltiel is reassured. But is this an advantage in his situation? Wouldn't it be better to be all mixed up, or for his memory to be blank? No. Anything is better than chaos or amnesia.

So what does Maimonides say?

"No commandment surpasses the one concerning the liberation of hostages, for they are among the starving, the thirsting, the stripped, always in danger of death."

In other words: If he, Shaltiel, has been abducted, the Jews of New York and Jerusalem are morally and legally obliged to pay whatever is demanded of them.

As his thoughts wander in the nebulous future, Shaltiel draws away from the physician philosopher of Cordoba and latches on to a visionary from Galilee. Specifically, he focuses on the decision in the *Shulchan Aruch,* or *Guide to Behavior,* by the famous Rabbi Joseph Karo of Safed in the fifteenth century: Even the building of a study house or synagogue should be stopped for the deliverance of a prisoner. Every delay is tantamount to a murder.

Shaltiel likes this mystic and his celestial dreams. A great

Sage took the trouble of coming down from the heavens to teach him the secrets of Creation in his sleep. I'm lucky, the hostage says to himself. My dreams are wounds; his were made of light. Could he assist me in my nightmare here?

Be careful, Shaltiel says to himself. Let's not run too fast. I need to stop and catch my breath to probe my memories from yesterday. But when was yesterday? And where? In what school? There was the Maharam of Rothenburg. Arrested in 1286, he tried to escape from Germany but was sentenced and imprisoned. From his cell, he sent his decision to the Jewish community: Do not pay a ransom, for it would encourage other abductions. He drew his last breath in jail, after seven years of captivity.

But then, if a shining light like the Maharam, one of Israel's Sages, the author of essential volumes on the foundation of religion, had to be abandoned to his fate, why would anyone care about a minor Jewish storyteller like me, who has only jotted down a few simple words on paper, a few sad and entertaining stories here and there, which probably no one has ever read, much less remembers?

Caution, Shaltiel. You're going offtrack. You're becoming too impassioned. Memory, which lurches forward and backward, has its own traps, its own breaks and cracks. You're tracing concentric circles, keeping yourself continually in the center. If you think too much about yourself, how will you stand up to future questioning? So, Nirvana no longer appeals to you? Dissolve the self in order to remain whole. This is not a Jewish attitude, true, but for the time being, the point is to survive. Isn't everything allowed in order to defeat death? Don't you want to live for those close to you, to take part in their joys and to help the new generation of young people struggle against the demons that assail them?

He decides to take a different approach. In his mind he lines up the men and women whose paths crossed his, and questions them about what to do or not to do in his situation.

His father, with a solemn air, advises him to stand fast. His stepmother says he should be careful and not give in to despair. His brother advises him to play deaf and dumb. One-Eyed Paritus says he should laugh even through tears. The musician from Kraków urges that he guard the tremulous song that haunts him.

Shaltiel questions them: Why this suffering? What is the meaning of this ordeal? Could it be a punishment for something? Could it be for having said too much, or not enough, in my stories? Or again—and nothing could be worse—for having said it badly? He doesn't realize that the torturer scores a victory over his victim when the latter, in the grip of doubt, begins to torture himself.

Torture is the act of making someone die a slow death, making the prisoner die several times.

Thoughts arise in the hostage's tormented brain. In the hospital, patients feel they are returning to childhood; in prison, they age. The gods blind themselves.

Shaltiel remembers a story:

A very young child is dreaming. I want to grow up, I want to sing of the joy of the world, I want to celebrate the dark beauty of the mountains, I want to kiss a woman, the most beautiful woman in the world, but . . .

"But what?" asks his would-be girlfriend.

"But I don't know how," says the little boy.

So she caresses his hair, his lips, his eyelids, which she closes, and says to him: Come, I'll show you how.

And his heart, the little boy's heart, begins beating violently. And the young woman's too.

Shaltiel, though prone to migraines, has never before awakened with such a bad headache. Even his teeth are throbbing. And he feels as though he were inside a heated iron vise. Is it just a nightmare? He's in pitch darkness. His hands and ankles are tied, his body numb. Moving his head, formulating an image, are painful. Everything aches. Just keeping his senses alert so that nothing will escape him is an exhausting effort. He's short of breath and his head is empty. He's alive, that's already something. He remembers Yankel, a survivor, who used to say to him, "When I wake up in the morning and have no aches and pains, I wonder if I'm still alive." Shaltiel doesn't wonder. Voices come to him from very close, amplifying his pain. Questions are burning his lips, but he knows they will be hard to answer. His mouth is swollen. What a predicament, he thinks. One day, I'll have to write a short story about it.

"Where am I?" he stammers.

Exhaustion has caused him to forget everything.

"Far away," says a voice.

The European accent gives him a start: Is he dreaming?

"Who are you?"

"None of your business."

"I have a right to know."

"We couldn't care less about your rights."

"Why am I here?"

"To help us."

"But who are you?"

"You know that already: We're freedom fighters."

The accent is guttural; it's the Arab.

"I can't help you. I'm Jewish," says Shaltiel, more in a dream than reality.

"What other revelations do you have for us?"

"I'm Jewish. My name is Shaltiel Feigenberg."

"As though we didn't know."

"I'm the son of Jews. The descendant of Abraham, Isaac and Jacob. The disciple of Moses, Isaiah and . . ."

The Arab slaps him on the right cheek.

"We're fighting for the liberation of Palestine. Keep your history lessons for your own people."

"So tell me why I'm here."

Another slap, on the left cheek. This is not a dream.

"Did you really forget everything?"

"I have a dreadful headache."

"You're here precisely because you're Jewish."

Oddly enough, Shaltiel feels slightly reassured. He had been trying lately to imagine the irrational, absurd fear that his father must have felt during the war, far away, over there.

He hears his abductors opening the two books he had borrowed from the library and had under his arm when they captured him; then he hears them throw them on the ground. They empty his pockets—a few dollars, a handkerchief, his library card.

"Why do you refuse to help us?" the Italian asks.

*Godlike
quality*

"I'm a storyteller. If you want, I'll tell you a story."

"Storyteller isn't a profession."

The Arab cuts in. "Where we come from, it is. Arab story-tellers are respected. But you're Jewish. Do Jews also respect them?"

"That depends on the storytellers."

"You," asks the Italian, "are you respected?"

"I respect those who listen to me," says Shaltiel.

"Do you also write your stories down?"

"It all depends on the stories. Some I write down."

Another slap from the Arab.

"Tell me," says the Italian, "do you know any wealthy and influential people?"

"The only wealth I'm interested in is a wealth of words. The people I know are different, you might say."

"Different in what way?"

"Today's wealthy are poor though they don't know it. They can't bring their possessions to where we're all going."

Shaltiel feels he has less to fear from the Italian than the Arab. The Italian must have doubts about this exploit. He must have some education; he must know Nietzsche, Hölder-lin, Wittgenstein. He must know that philosophers don't turn into executioners; they're incapable of it. A crazy and slightly ridiculous idea surfaces in his seething mind: In other circum-stances, could they have become friends? And what about in these circumstances? Oh my heavens, the famous Stockholm syndrome! Oh no, says the prisoner to himself, not that.

"I imagine you've published some of your stories," says Luigi.

"Yes," says Shaltiel. "But very few."

"In what language?"

"In Hebrew, in Yiddish and in English. But I also speak French."

"Where could I find them? I mean the writings in English."

"In the New York Public Library. In fact, if you want, I'd be glad to go there with you."

The Arab shouts an obscenity and punches him for the first time. "Oh, and he thinks he's being funny!"

And he thinks he's a revolutionary! Shaltiel says to himself, surprised that he's beginning to collect his thoughts again.

A face flashes before the prisoner's swollen eyes: *Piotr. Where are you, my friend? Come and help me!*

The torturers interrupt the session. They're not getting anywhere.

Revolution, thinks Shaltiel, it's a noble concept, but a blood-drenched word. Its results are violence and transformation. It sparks the most human hope and the cruelest loss of hope—Robespierre and Saint-Just, Lenin and Trotsky, Bakunin and Stalin; scaffolds, guillotines, jails, the Gulag, concentration camps.

With the years and convulsions of history, the word—as reductionist as the dictionary itself—has undergone absurd metamorphoses. In some countries, they prefer the word "destabilization." "Poor" countries no longer exist, just "disad-vantaged" or "underprivileged" ones. We say "brainwashing" instead of "propaganda." And now we refer to revolutions in fashion, music and electronics, where ink flows but not blood. The point is profit, not truth.

Shaltiel remembers the "1968 Revolution." He was spending a few weeks alone in Paris; Blanca had to take her exams in New York. In Germany, America, England—everywhere—young people were in rebellion, eager for change, every type of change. In Paris, the students occupied the Sorbonne; in New York, they invaded Columbia University. The postwar generation berated its recent history. It had had more than enough of the wealthy class, the overlords, the decision-makers.

Shaltiel was happy. He was giddy with hope, exhilarated by life and humanity. The enthusiasm in the Latin Quarter, the rioting—it was like a celebration. A celebration of freedom, of happiness. Strangers kissed each other, vowing eternal love that lasted only an hour, an instant, a glimmer. There was magnificent sexual liberation. It was forbidden to forbid. The power of imagination and imagination in power! Long live anarchy, the liberator!

It was a struggle of the "people" against authority, battling the establishment, repudiating everything that had been taken for granted, accepted, respected and admired. The police, the tear gas—driven back, the students came back yelling, chanting, laughing. Idols were abolished, glories repudiated. Friends, it was said, let's start all over again, from Creation! Down with the rich, the great, the master thinkers, comrades! Down with matter, long live poetry!

Shaltiel had joined the crowd. Sometimes he didn't know why they were fighting or whom they were denouncing. He hadn't mastered French, but he felt at home among friends and accomplices on the Boulevard Saint-Germain. He didn't really understand what he saw, but he participated in it with a juvenile enthusiasm.

Oh, to sing the praises of the body and its areas of mystery—that was called loving. Suddenly everything became possible, vivid and within reach. They were at the seat of action. It was a destructive novel of acquired ideas. To finally wake up in a state of creative anguish, to lose oneself in order to find oneself again, to sleep in the arms of a beautiful student whose name one didn't know, to fall back to sleep over a love poem—that was called existence. The harmonics of artistic creation, of fertile sensibility, of anticipated events—history in movement—that was called a privilege.

A happy, peaceful man is walking in the street, holding two books. Some strangers seize him and imprison him. That is called a hostage taking.

He had remained faithful to Blanca, in his own way. She had continued to exist in his mind. Even when his body was overwhelmed by desire, his passion went to her.

Yes, he had lived through those events in Paris. They were still inscribed in his flesh and his conscience, embedded in his inner self, the underpinning and crucible of frustrations and emotions that were beyond him. And to think he might be leaving this earth without having had the time to transform them into stories.

No one had died in those clashes. And here these two terrorists, these torturers, enthusiasts of murder, dared to call themselves revolutionaries! Danton, Robespierre, Saint-Just—these disciples of yours may have kept their heads, but they have lost their hearts and souls. They have rediscovered idolatry.

.   .   .

Shaltiel thinks of his father. Their story is made up of so many chapters and revelations. If the executioners bring him down, they will kill his father as well.

Shaltiel draws from his memories:

An emaciated, famished and exhausted man lies in a bed in a military hospital. Haskel Feigenberg is convinced that all his relatives have perished except Arele, his nephew, and his son Pinhas, in Russia. His parents, his brothers and sisters, his uncles, aunts, cousins—all have died. Some of them together, on the same night, upon arriving at the camp, during the first selection.

In his feverish, ailing brain, Shaltiel tries to visualize his father's face, no doubt changed by beatings and blows. How did he manage to survive for so long? Was Death just too busy elsewhere?

Shaltiel recalls what his father had recounted: the evacuation from the camp, the night march through snow flurries and a violent wind. Guttural howls of "Faster, faster." Cracking. Whistling. Pistol and rifle shots. In an ocher, pallid, repulsive light, dry, hard noises; bodies deformed by hunger, fear, decrepitude and the remnants of an empty, disfigured life. Some slow up, exhausted. Comrades cry out to them not to slow up; they must not. Whoever is separated from the crowd, whoever doesn't keep walking, is shot. Haskel is losing his strength. He clings to one unknown comrade and another, all winded stragglers like he. A few more steps. Still a few more. The barking of dogs. Forward, forward. As though Death were at their heels.

Haskel is no longer running or making progress. He doesn't

know where he is anymore, or where he's going. He walks gropingly. Then he stops walking, falls into a ditch with others who have reached their limit. What's the point of wanting to live if life is a traveling slaughterhouse?

Machine guns shoot into the night and its ghosts. Snow is a cemetery. Haskel passes out. But he doesn't die. No bullet has entered his body. Hours go by. The day dawns on many corpses lying in a strangely peaceful landscape. Someone shakes Haskel: "Wake up if you're still alive!" The hoarse words come to him from afar. "You're moving, so you're alive," the same voice says, booming. While lying in the snow, Haskel makes a superhuman effort and opens his eyelids. It's Leibele. They had become friends in the camp. Now he's a fellow orphan, famished, weakened, marked for death. As they labored, they had exchanged Hasidic sayings and stories: the ones from Vizhnitz for those from Guer. What was he doing here, stepping over corpses, all awaiting burial under the heavy, huge, silvery snowflakes? "You're alive, thank God," says Leibele. "Pull yourself together. Get up. Let's not stay here. The SS are gone, but they may come back; you never know. We're the last ones, the only ones."

Haskel, his limbs numb, gets up unsteadily, helped by his friend. Where should they go? Leibele thinks they should return to the camp. At least then they'll know where they are. Haskel replies that it's too far away; he doesn't have the strength. Leibele tells him to take his arm. Remaining where they are, he thinks, is exposing themselves to death.

Two desperate young old men stagger forward, with small steps, nearly sliding, toward a more uncertain future than opaque slumber.

After wandering aimlessly for hours, Leibele spots a hut in

the distance. An old peasant woman wearing a black headscarf opens the door for them and ushers them in. The heat smacks them in the face. Dazed, they collapse on the beaten-earth floor. They think they're in paradise.

The peasant woman crosses herself and hands them some warm milk. She talks to them in Polish. Leibele understands her. He translates in a whisper: "The Germans have left, but if they come back they'll kill all of us, including her. But she's not afraid . . . at her age. And besides, the village is expecting the Russians, who are very near."

They stay with her. Haskel will never forget her. Nor will he ever forget his friend.

The Russians arrived a week later on a beautiful, peaceful day. Four armed soldiers suddenly appeared in front of the hut and stiffened. They looked around inquisitively and spoke among themselves for a while. Then one of them opened the door without knocking, pointing his cocked rifle in front of him. The old woman, with no trace of fear, said to him, in Polish, to come in and warm up. He paid her no heed, turning instead to the two young human skeletons and yelling, "And you, who are you? Hands up!" The old woman was about to answer, but Leibele spoke first. "We're from over there." With his right hand, he pointed to the rear. The soldier looked him over and then glanced at Haskel: Standing motionless, the two men smiled at him faintly and pitifully, as if to welcome him. The soldier called out to his comrades. "Look, Ilya," he said to the eldest of the four, "you who are Jewish, take a good look at them and tell them the Red Army is happy and proud to be bringing them liberation and life."

Ilya said a few words to Haskel that Leibele translated. They had just seen the camp. There were still a few survivors, who were being treated by military physicians. "And you," he said to Haskel, "where are you from?"

Haskel replied that he was from Galicia.

"But you're Jewish, aren't you?"

"Yes. Jewish."

"You speak Yiddish?"

"Yes, I do. I've spoken it all my life." Thereupon Ilya started chatting with them in the language that had almost been silenced forever by Hitler's madness.

Ilya and one of his comrades took off their padded jackets and slung them over the backs of the two survivors. They left the old peasant woman after having given her all the food in their possession.

Haskel and Leibele were taken to a refugee center in Kraków but fell ill there with high fevers. Ilya took them to a military hospital and put them in the care of warmhearted personnel. The two friends lay side by side, each locked in his own pain.

Haskel was the first to get better. A young army nurse feeding him some hot tea told him in Yiddish that her name was Natasha and that she was happy to report he was doing much better. He couldn't believe it, he said. She smiled and caressed his forehead. The nurse spoke Yiddish! he thought to himself. What was she doing at his bedside, and how did she know he too spoke Yiddish?

She seemed to read his thoughts. "Ilya told me about you

and Leibele." She paused for a moment, then added, "You'll be fine, you'll live, I promise. You can count on Ilya and me." She looked around to make sure no one could hear her, then went on, "After all, we're Jewish. You suffered enormously. We must help one another." Natasha was Jewish; the thought reassured him.

"What about my friend?" he asked. "Where is he? Why isn't he here with me? How is he?"

The young woman's face darkened.

"He's not well. I'm sorry to have to tell you; he's not well at all. It's hard to fight it, but we're trying, believe me. A miracle is always possible."

Natasha didn't want to drive him to despair; that was clear.

"A miracle? Did you use the word 'miracle'?"

"Yes, I did. You never know. Ilya tells me you come from a religious family. Is that true?"

"Yes, it's true. Very religious."

"Then pray for him."

Pray? Haskel said to himself, I haven't addressed prayers to the God of my ancestors for ages. I've been telling myself that a Sage should invent new ones, prayers that no mouth has pronounced yet, prayers that would bear the burning stamp of an accursed place called Auschwitz.

"I'd like to see my friend," he said to the nurse.

"Why?"

"If what you say is true, my friend will be leaving us soon. I'd like to be present."

"But you're not well yet, Haskel. You won't be able to stand up."

"Yes I will. I'm strong enough, you'll see. I must see him. Please, Natasha, please help two Jewish friends to get together for the last time."

Natasha looked at her watch.

"Ilya will be here very soon. I'll discuss it with him." She left him.

For the first time since his deportation, Haskel's eyes filled with tears. Over there, people didn't cry, for they feared they would never be able to stop. Now he would have to make an effort not to break down if he got to see his dying friend one last time.

Natasha and Ilya arrived, forced smiles on their lips. Ilya sat down at the edge of the bed.

"Listen, Haskel, my friend, I know you can be strong; proof is, you're here, among us. Here's what I suggest: In a few hours we'll go with you to Leibele's room. You'll stay for no more than fifteen minutes, and then you'll come back here. Agreed?"

Haskel nodded yes.

It was a long, irritating wait. His nerves were on edge. He didn't want to answer questions as to his own health. He had no appetite; it was hard for him to swallow. He thought of praying, remembering those he had known in his childhood. Should he pray for his wife? How could he know if . . . ? So as not to think about them, he prayed for Redemption in the distant future and happiness in the near future. He prayed for health, peace, springtime, bread and honey: No tradition has as many entreaties and divine interventions. Were all of them in vain? God may have turned away.

In the late afternoon, Natasha and Ilya took him to the

room opposite his. There was just one bed and Leibele was in it. His face was bathed in sweat, his body shaking with convulsions, his lips trembling—he seemed delirious.

"Leibele, my friend," said Haskel in a very low voice.

There was no reply.

"It's me, Haskel. Can you hear me?"

No response.

Haskel didn't dare scream, but he certainly wanted to, at the top of his voice.

He wanted to wake up his friend, keep him alive, have him stay with him for another hour, for eternity. But Leibele couldn't hear anything.

Haskel wished he could touch him, or get close to him, but his two chaperones wouldn't let him. So he had to content himself with leaning closer to the patient.

"Leibele, Leibele, I want to pray for you. I have to know your mother's name, Leibele; tell me your mother's name."

As Leibele started mumbling something, Natasha stifled a small cry, her hand over her mouth.

"He's talking to me," Haskel cried out, with joy.

He began moving closer to the patient, but Ilya stopped him. He put a white handkerchief over his mouth.

"Go ahead, my friend," said Ilya. "But only for a minute."

Haskel bent over his friend's parchment-like face and heard him whisper, "My mother's name . . . is Rachel, Rochele. My mother's . . . name is Rochele."

Haskel straightened up and stepped back.

"God of Abraham, Isaac and Jacob, among all your sick, heal Leib, son of Rachel, of all his ills."

"My mother," Leibele said in a trembling whisper, "she

left before me. She's waiting for me up there. And I'm waiting for her."

He knows, Haskel said to himself. The anguish he felt was almost overwhelming.

"You're going to get well, Leibele. I promise in the name of my dear ones. We're going to study together, pray together, tell the world about the dangers of forgetting . . . together."

"Yes, yes, my friend . . . Haskel. My mother . . ."

He was drawing nearer to her, that was certain. Soon he would be with her, just as Haskel would one day be with *his* mother. A tear trickled down his cheek.

Suddenly, Leibele tried to lift himself up. As his eyes met Haskel's, his speech became stronger.

"If your prayer is answered, the first thing I'll do is pray with you. I'll wear tefillin and so will you."

He fell back on the drenched pillow. He was drifting away.

Natasha looked at him tenderly. Months later, after she and Ilya had to return to the Soviet Union, Ilya asked her to marry him. The last time Haskel saw Ilya, he asked his Russian savior to get him a pair of tefillin.

Shaltiel has discovered that his worst enemy is not his memory overflowing with events and faces, or his exacerbated sensitivity, but his body, his whole body, strained and enfeebled. The Arab torturer is weakening Shaltiel's resistance and undermining his spirit by punishing his body. Deprived of food and sleep, his eyelids are as heavy as lead. His tongue sticks to his palate. His lips are gashed. His head and lungs are bursting. He has shooting pains in his shoulders, hands and fingers. Breathing is an ordeal.

Is it daylight outside or dusk? He'd very much like to know, though it really doesn't matter. He doesn't know anything, except that hell exists.

"Confess, you louse!" the Arab commands. "You're Jewish, you're a spy, you belong to a criminal group. Confess that you support your Jewish brothers in Palestine, that you love them, the murderers of my people. We know it."

He has lowered his voice, as if people on the street outside might hear him. There is daylight now. The hostage strains to hear noise from the outside—any noise from a cityscape that is no longer.

Shaltiel nods his head, his nose covered in blood. Yes, he says, he loves the people of Israel, but, no, he's never been a threat to the Palestinians. From where does he get his courage? Is it because he's innocent? He doesn't know. He only knows, between two fainting fits, that the Arab is torturing him and that torturers are never right. Worse than the physical suffering is the powerlessness in the face of humiliation. Still, it's his body that's subjecting him to humiliation. The penetrating stench of the urine and the vomit. He is like a child again, unable to control himself. His head is throbbing and his heart aches as he is trapped in a world that repudiates him. With a bleeding mouth, he blurts it all out again. Yes, yes he's Jewish! Yes, he tries to write and tell stories! Yes, he's been to the Holy Land—but only to visit cousins in Jerusalem, and to pray; yes, to pray at the Wall, and cry, and dream. That's all.

But the torturer is not satisfied: "That's not enough!" He splits open the arch of Shaltiel's eyebrows with his fist.

His eyesight seems to have changed. He doesn't see the shadows, yet he feels their ominous presence. He guesses about everything, but understands nothing.

When it's the Italian's turn, things are more tolerable; he knows the two men are playing good cop, bad cop. Still, the European seems to be interested in his parents, his wife, his occupations.

One day, he says to him, "Since you say you're a storyteller, tell me a story."

"I can't."

"Why not?"

"My mouth is too dry."

The Italian gives him a drink. But Shaltiel still can't. He can't concentrate.

Finally, in a rasping voice, between two sighs, Shaltiel tells his abductor the story of the wise bird.

One day, God decided to send a special messenger to earth to put his creatures back on the straight and narrow path. He sent a bird, a tiny, very beautiful and fragile bird. The bird dared to plead that he was too small, too weak and too ignorant for the assignment. He was bound to lose his way, bound to be insulted and beaten. God reassured him: "Don't worry, my little messenger. I'll be at your side all the time, everywhere. You won't have to talk; you have the gift of song, so you'll sing for them. When they speak to you, it's me that they'll hear."

The confident bird now left the heavens and flew down to the earth. He arrived at the house of sleeping merchants, where his singing woke them up. They chased him away. "They're so exhausted buying and selling things they'll never own that their eyes shut involuntarily," God said to the bird. "Don't resent them. They're not guilty of sleeping but of not understanding."

The bird, as he flew, noticed an army getting ready for combat. "How could I possibly sing?" he asks God. "They want to kill and die; they love murder." God told him to sing nonetheless. The bird obeyed. Only one soldier heard him, and that man threw a stone at him. God, as though hurt, uttered a small cry and the soldier collapsed.

Later, as the messenger bird was resting in a fruit tree, he saw a little boy and his old grandfather looking at him, and he heard them praise his grace and beauty. He wanted to thank them, but God told him to remain silent. "It's for them that I made you fly down. I'd like to teach you something useful and true: Your silence should be a song, a song so solemn and timeless that it will silence forever hatred and bloodthirstiness in the hearts of mortals."

"He's not here," said Shaltiel's captor. "Your little bird doesn't live here. Haven't you understood yet? Here your silence, like everything else, like everything in life, will just be one long howl."

He was right, of course.

And yet, without knowing why, Shaltiel thought of his older brother, whose silences touched his.

Davarowsk-the-great-Podolsk: the small town in Galicia where an ordinary Jewish family lived, amid others, honoring the religious customs and attending to its daily worries. They observed the Sabbath and the High Holy Days and visited friends. There was very little talk about politics at the dinner table. There were no daughters but three brothers: Pinhas or Pavel, Berele and Shaltiel.

It was the father, Reb Haskel, a peddler of ancient and modern books, who saw to the running of the household. Bread, milk and a few seasonal fruits were usually served; rarely warm dishes. For the Sabbath meals, a proper effort was made to honor the day's holiness.

As Reb Haskel's salary was very low, he supplemented it by tutoring the children of the wealthy on the sacred texts. In addition, in the evening, in his spare time, as an amateur scribe, he corrected the parchments of the phylacteries under the supervision of a professional.

Berele, the youngest boy, died at age five. Shaltiel remembers his death, but only vaguely. He remembers his funeral more vividly. Rain fell on the open tomb, and Shaltiel was tormented with the thought that his little brother was going to be drenched and all alone. People cried as his father recited the Kaddish.

The bereaved family knew periods of poverty. At night, they often rose from the dinner table with half-empty stomachs. But the father was determined that his children would not give way to melancholy. A funny story, a kind word from him sufficed to chase away sadness. When he had to leave home, even for a day, he invariably told his children to respect their mother and remember that one day they would no longer be here to guide them, but they must remain together, always.

The eldest son, Pinhas, had a strenuous job in a sawmill. There, at sixteen, he discovered the Communist ideal and experiment. Arele, Haskel's nephew, found his path to God at fourteen and turned to mysticism at eighteen. As for Shaltiel, he was fascinated by chess and devoted all his free time to the game; he also cultivated all the passions that would haunt him: the desire to understand others, a faith in history—not blind history but history with a human face—anger when confronted with the unexpected, an awareness of time passing. Even in his jail, he tried to slow its course in order to escape from pain and anguish by playing difficult games.

"In a certain way, our three destinies remained strangely linked," Shaltiel would later say. "It was because Pavel was a Communist that Arele became interested in religion and me, in the spellbinding world of chess."

A man's life, really, is not made up of years but of moments, all of which are fertile and unique. This is what I was taught by an old man who begged for words and stories, and I never tire of repeating his lesson. Some of life's moments mark a break in consciousness; others give rise to streams of scintillating, philosophical ideas or astonishing works of art; still others, to important meetings or profound personal upheavals.

When exactly did Pinhas, my dear older brother, get the revelatory summons from Moscow? That's something that no one at home knew except for me. Perhaps he told me because he was fond of me. I was still a little boy when he left home. In order to protect himself and probably so we wouldn't have problems with the police, he didn't tell us about his membership in the clandestine Jewish Communist Party for a long time. He was frequently absent at night, but he told my father he was only meeting with friends. Did my father suspect the truth? He did know how to read our thoughts without ever passing judgment on them. So long as his sons gathered at the table for the Sabbath meal, and so long as they went to synagogue with him on the Sabbath and on the High Holy Days, he didn't mind. However, as Pinhas spoke very little about his nocturnal occupations, our curiosity kept growing. Until the day he confided his great secret to Arele: He was in love. Not with a brunette or a blonde, but with a revolutionary movement that promised to give humanity a sunny, fulfilling future.

An older comrade at the sawmill, Zelig, who was financially even worse off than he, a courageous young man whose irony was as remarkable as his physical strength, was responsible for his conversion. He had gone about it slowly and methodically. First, through incisive little remarks, Zelig undermined his candidate's religious faith, demonstrating to him that the heavens were as empty as they were deceptive. Marx replaced Moses. Stalin outclassed the Messiah.

At first, Pinhas resisted.

"You don't believe in God, that's your business," he said to Zelig. "Not mine. I believe in Him just like my father, though it's true that in his observance, he is more scrupulous than I; I sometimes forget to bless my bread or fruit before eating it, and sometimes I also pray hastily without trying to understand the meaning of the words. But I believe God exists."

"But do you exist for Him?" Zelig asked. "That is the question."

"My answer is yes, I do, and so do you. Think what you will; we exist for God. He didn't create the world in order to get rid of it!"

"And what makes you think He created our world and the human beings who populate it? Don't you understand that it's not God who created us but we who invented God! Science is here to prove it."

Unfortunately, Pinhas did not have the intellectual background to refute his comrade's dialectical materialism. True, he could have turned to our father. He was erudite; he could have helped and suggested the appropriate books for him to read. But Pinhas thought his father might see it as challenging his faith and that it would make him sad. He preferred to keep silent.

Actually, he was wrong. Our father would have known what to answer. He would have told him the story of the great author of *Hatam Sofer* whose young son asked him a question concerning the faith. The father took a week to answer him. "Can it be," the son asked, "that you needed so much time to find the answer to my question?"

"No," his father replied. "I could have given you the answer right away. But I wanted you to understand this: People can easily live solely with questions; and also you should know that some questions remain forever unanswered."

But Pavel needed answers and he pursued them. Sometimes at the sawmill the two young Jews would have discussions—about the origin of the universe, manhood, the enigma of free will in the divine design, the tragic sentiment of life and, more tragic, of death. How could these things be explained? Zelig had an answer for everything. Always pressing ahead, he drove his friend into a corner: "If your God knows everything, then you're not free; and if you have no freedom, then you're not responsible for anything; but then why fear divine punishment?"

Pinhas's inexperience made his friend, who was so very knowledgeable, ill at ease. So he suggested a deal: They would no longer talk about philosophy or religion, but would devote themselves to analyzing political and social problems. Eventually, they came to communism, its importance to Jews first, and then to all peoples.

"Communism is the ultimate remedy for anguish, injustice, evil, hatred, anti-Semitism and war," said Zelig.

"Prove it," said Pinhas.

"Gladly. In the world we live in, you and I, everything is going badly. The rich exploit the defenseless and the downtrodden. Why? Because communism doesn't rule here yet."

"But where does it rule then?"

"In the Soviet Union, the true home of all stateless persons," Zelig replied.

"How did you come to all these ideas?"

"Through books, of course. And from Communists, of

course. One day you'll understand: Communism is a conception of the world; it encompasses all our aspirations and offers us all possibilities."

Night after night, Zelig and Pinhas discussed historical materialism, the imperative of the dialectic and the meaning of history. Zelig described the Communist paradise as defined in the Soviet constitution. And he based his arguments on clandestine Yiddish brochures that confirmed his statements. In fact, these brochures also alluded to a kind of independent Jewish state called Birobidzhan where everyone would be Jewish and Yiddish would be spoken by everyone, from its leaders to its ordinary citizens, and used in official publications and newspapers. In other words, no more anti-Semitism. No more threats. No more danger. Happiness would be shared by all; pure joy would reign at all levels, everywhere. No one would feel useless or inferior. No one would say: I'm better than you. No one would have the power or the right to humiliate or exploit anyone, in the name of anything.

"Imagine a world," Zelig said, "where all men are equal, where racial hatred and religious fanaticism are replaced by a great human solidarity. Your father wouldn't work as hard nor would you. The Jews wouldn't be persecuted and the poor wouldn't die of hunger."

"You're describing the Messianic era," said Pinhas.

"Yes. But it will be created by men, not gods."

One night, Pinhas adopted a solemn expression and asked, "What do you expect of me?"

There was a silence, and then Zelig answered, "Become a Communist. Like me. With me."

For Pinhas, this moment was a turning point.

His first appearance before the Peretz Markish cell, named after the great poet living in Moscow, was memorable and dramatic. It felt like a complete upheaval in his life. The cell consisted of seven members, five men and two women. Pavel was the youngest. The secretary, Gregory, a dry and taciturn bald man who took himself very seriously, dominated the evening, with short, solemn sermons directed at the new revolutionary.

"We're pleased to welcome you into our movement. We're accepting you because your supporter is a comrade whom we trust. We hope you won't disappoint us. Be sure to observe all the security rules scrupulously. We're operating in a hostile atmosphere. We're spied on by informers. The police are always seeking us out, aware of the danger we represent for the people they protect. All your ties to us must remain secret. Not one word to anyone, not even to the people closest to you."

After a pause, he looked at Pavel with a searching and stern gaze and added, "From now on, your family is us. We have complete priority over all the people who are not party members. Forget your individual conscience and your personal passions: You've now written them off once and for all. The party is the equivalent of God for your father: the beginning and end of all things. Betray the party and you'll be damned."

They all nodded their heads. The young convert had been warned. Evil exists, and it is betrayal.

Though a good Communist, faithful to the ideals of Marx and Stalin, Pinhas remained a good Jew, in part because he was a good son. He didn't want to upset our father, so he went to great lengths not to change his way of life.

As I said, I don't know why, but he chose me as his confidant. And it's he who first taught me chess, when I was still little; I played with my father only later. One day, while we were playing, he told me the story of a young boy, an occasional magician, who devoted his life to a noble conspiracy: making history move forward and rescuing human beings from despair. Afterward, he referred to him often though making it clear that he was an imaginary character. His faith in the future became his gateway to a romantic circle of initiates all linked to a gigantic worldwide fraternity. He constantly came within a hairsbreadth of danger; ran the risk of being identified, imprisoned and beaten; felt the excitement of distributing forbidden tracts under the doors of Jewish homes and outwitting the police. And then came the harrowing but also thrilling preparation of the use of violence.

Whom was he speaking of, if not himself and his dreams?

Yet he led an open and ordered life as before. He was never absent from his place of work. He never criticized his employers. He celebrated the Sabbath and the holidays with us.

Only once did he have to deal with a snag. His cell had decided to meet on a Sabbath evening. How could he justify not being present at the Friday evening meal? He invented a friend's illness. Father wanted to know how serious his friend's condition was, and Pinhas, a bad liar, gave an answer that was too vague to be convincing. Nevertheless, my older brother's seat stayed empty for the Sabbath meal.

That night the offices of the police were set on fire. A young Jew was arrested; dangerous pamphlets were found in his home. He confessed under torture that he was a Communist. He mentioned Pinhas's cell, and the secretary was immediately apprehended and cross-examined. The others were obliged to hide, in the mountains, or elsewhere. Pinhas decided to spend a few days with a distant cousin. Father wanted to know why. Pinhas tried to dodge the question. Father demanded the truth and Pinhas confessed: He was involved in the conspiracy. "So you're mixed up in the fire?" asked my father, alarmed.

"Not directly."

"What does that mean, not directly? Is that yes or no? If yes, in what way?" Lowering his eyes, Pinhas acknowledged his membership in the Jewish Communist Party, emphasizing the word "Jewish." Father reflected at length before giving his opinion: "Then you're in danger. Go quickly to your cousin's house."

At dawn the next morning the police came to our house intending to take Pinhas into custody. They combed the house from top to bottom looking for arms, explosives or subversive propaganda, but they found nothing. Questioned separately, each of us gave the same answer: Pinhas often visited friends in Debrecen, Hungary, for a few days' rest.

Years later, Pinhas told me how tormented he had been: What if the police had taken one of us hostage? What would he have done?

Zelig, who was also safely hidden away, contacted Pinhas through a reliable go-between and told him that he had received the consent of the party's secret service to leave for the Soviet Union: Being too well known in Davarowsk, Zelig was putting all the cells in danger. Zelig asked the proper authorities if he could bring his companion Pavel, whose party loyalty he could vouch for. Twenty-four hours later, the party responded affirmatively.

Zelig organized a last family reunion in a safe hideaway at the edge of the forest. Dressed like a peasant, Pinhas seemed both anguished and excited. He promised my father that when he got to Russia he would arrange to have us all join him. We would live without fear over there. Father listened to him, distraught, and said, "I don't know when we'll be seeing each other again, son. But take your tefillin. They'll protect you. And . . ."

"Yes, Father?

"Never forget that you're Jewish."

"I won't forget, Father."

Pinhas kissed his hand, and I thought I saw tears in his eyes.

Suddenly, my father pulled himself together and said, "I almost forgot—since you're going to Russia, you should know that we have family in Moscow."

Pinhas was surprised.

"Make sure you remember his name. He's a Communist too. His name is Leon Meirovitch. He's a close collaborator of Lazar Kaganovich."

"I'll remember," Pinhas said.

In the course of their trip, Pinhas mentioned the name of his relative to Zelig. The latter gave a start, as if he'd been stung by a bee.

"What? What did you just say? You have a relative who is a close collaborator of Kaganovich, Lazar Kaganovich? Are you sure?"

"Yes. That's what my father told me."

Zelig was convinced that Pavel and his father were mistaken; they couldn't possibly have a relative who really worked with Kaganovich, one of Stalin's closest collaborators. And yet they did.

Press excerpts: October 27, 1975

The Washington Post, Washington, D.C.
Shaltiel Feigenberg, who was recently taken hostage in
New York, is from an Orthodox Jewish family. He has
no children. It is still unclear why he has been taken
hostage.

Al-Ahram, Cairo
The Jew Shaltiel Feigenberg, who was abducted by a
nationalist Palestinian group in New York, is a young
Zionist, known for his activities in support of the Jewish state. Many Muslims in the Arab world applaud the
abduction as an act of protest against the Jewish occupation of Palestine.

Le Figaro, Paris
We have learned that the Jewish-American Shaltiel
Feigenberg, who was abducted in New York, lived in

France in the 1960s and completed a thesis on mysticism
at the Sorbonne. Investigators believe the abductors,
Palestinian extremists, may demand a ransom.

The Jerusalem Post, Jerusalem
The Israeli government is alarmed by the disappearance
of Shaltiel Feigenberg in the United States, given the
involvement of an underground Palestinian organization. It is very likely they will demand a ransom. Developments are being closely followed by the Mossad and
the Ministry of Foreign Affairs. According to one
high-ranking government official, the prime minister
believes that Israel is worried that similar incidents may
take place throughout the Jewish Diaspora.

Yedioth Ahronoth, Tel Aviv
Shaltiel Feigenberg is a young Jewish writer who has
published political-literary articles, some of which have
appeared in our columns. He has been missing from his
home in Brooklyn since yesterday. The police are col-
laborating with intelligence services both here and in
the United States.

The New York Times, New York
Shaltiel Feigenberg, born in Transylvania in 1935, lives
in Brooklyn with his wife, Blanca. They have no children. The couple met at New York University.

Is it his second or third day of captivity? Endless hours of thirst, hunger, tension, pain. Unable to see or to move. His thoughts wander as he seeks something to latch on to, something to help him avoid falling into the abyss.

One-Eyed Paritus materializes from the recesses of his mind. He could see farther than anyone. Where are you, my old friend and guide? Did you ever experience prison? Were you ever subjected to torture? Did you ever feel tempted by death?

The air is stifling. He wants to cry out, weep, vomit. It reminds him of his first sea journey, to the Far East. He was young and irresponsible, and felt the need to free himself from his habits and duties, from the anxieties of his kind father and the mysticism of his cousin Arele. He longed, in short, for a change in his everyday life. He wanted to look deeply into himself before surrendering to Blanca, to the sway of her love and passion, before handing her his freedom. Just then, to be without ties—that was what he wanted. Blanca had been understanding and shown no resentment. "Good idea," she said. "Distance will help you straighten out your thinking." In fact, on the ship, while feeling so ill, it was he who resented her. Why had she not shed a few tears, begged him to stay, kissed him? Why did she not protest, saying the decision was proof of his egoism, that he thought more about himself than about her? Like Job, he now felt lonelier than ever. And yet, just like Job, who had three friends keeping him company, at sea, Shaltiel always had someone by his side.

How could this "someone" be defined? Paritus is an ageless man. When he listens, he looks old, moderate and wise. When he speaks, he blazes with the intensity of youth. Where does his knowledge in so many areas come from? He must have had a full and turbulent life. Is he single? Is he married? Did he have the time or desire to start a family? Never surprised, he himself is surprising for his vast knowledge and experience. When he explains a passage from an ancient text, whether Jewish, Christian, Buddhist or secular, it's as though he had kept company with the author. To follow him, Shaltiel has to focus his attention.

I met him as I was on my way to the Far East. I had found a journalistic pretext. A Yiddish daily in New York suggested I try to find the traces of a Jewish kingdom in India, founded twelve centuries ago by the ten tribes exiled from Jerusalem by Sanheriv, the king of the Assyrians. I was twenty-four years old. I was no longer happy with my life. I had to find my bearings again, to renew myself. It was through Paritus and his book on personal and collective crises that I came to understand this.

The young noblemen in Persepolis had to learn to ride a horse, shoot an arrow and tell the truth. If you don't know what to do with your life and don't know how to ride or shoot an arrow, become a storyteller. You want to become a storyteller? It's more than a profession, more than a vocation; it's a mission and a revelation. To take it on, you must be capable of breaking all ties, of accepting a change of scene and going far away, as far away as possible, without necessarily moving from where you are. But that you'll discover later, only after having crossed the mountains and the oceans. Don't forget what you read: God created man and gave the storytellers the task of saying why.

On a completely different level, having always been attracted by the esoteric sciences and their mystery of mysteries, I was looking for an unfamiliar country or landscape where I could study mysticism.

I embarked on a ship in London, where I had gone to visit a distant cousin, and he, Paritus, embarked in Port Said, Egypt. When he walked into the small, somewhat dismal and dark third-class cabin, I was resentful: Even alone, I had felt cramped. And I was fond of my solitude.

Tall, untidy, bearded, a tanned face covered with wrinkles, he didn't even greet me with a nod; he set his worn and battered suitcase down on a chair and started to unpack—underwear, clothes, and especially books, which he threw in a jumble on the bed. I glanced indiscreetly at the pile: English, French, German, Yiddish, Hebrew and countless other languages. He's a Jewish intellectual, I thought to myself. Should I talk to him? I decided to wait. Would he introduce himself? Where does he come from? Where is he going? Why is he going to the Far

East? Is he running away like me? Is he trying to write like me? Will he disembark in Aden like Paul Nizan? Perhaps his behavior is meant to convey that he would rather keep his distance from inquisitive people. Bah, all for the better. Conversing with strangers was not my purpose when I decided to set out on this pilgrimage in search of a Jewish legend whose origins were obscure. So I affected to be reading a specialized journal. He walked out without saying a word.

I followed him up on deck, but not right away. Many people wanted to watch our departure. Under an unblemished blue spring sky, the cumbersome ship moved away from the land with a calculated, graceless, indifferent slowness. Whistles went off and people shouted. There was the usual hubbub on the dock. A mix of vendors, guides and beggars were hoping for profits and alms. Friends and families stood by as destinies separated. A mother was crying and waving her handkerchief. A man wearing sunglasses—her husband?—caressed her hair.

Of course, no one had come to bid me farewell. My true love, Blanca, was far away, in the New World. Was she thinking of me? Did she resent me for having abandoned her? Actually, why *had* I left her? Did I want to find out if she could be convinced, with time, to belong to another? Did I see myself as a thief of her soul? Had I left so I could delve into these questions? My morose, bizarre roommate had vanished into the crowd. Later, I found him back in the cabin. He had a book on his knees and was staring into space. I did not disturb him.

In the evening, he didn't come to dinner. Perhaps he was unwell with a migraine or an upset stomach. But why didn't he speak? I concluded he simply did not want to exchange meaningless words with a stranger. That was his privilege.

That night I slept badly. I was dreadfully seasick. My room-mate saw me running to the sink, yet he never asked me if he could do anything for me. In fact, he never said a word. He spent the night sitting bolt upright in his chair, his head buried in his book, his mind far away, living in his own world. Would he remain seated, unapproachable, impassive, until our arrival? Could he be a deaf-mute? From time to time, he expressed himself with nods and glances. I would have asked to change cabins, but they were all occupied.

Two days and two nights went by. I could not keep food down and suffered from a violent headache. Fortunately, my roommate wound up taking care of me. He brought me warm tea for my stomach and cold water for my burning forehead. Then, one morning, I woke up soothed; the sea had become calm. Soon, the ship put in at Aden. I went up on deck. Some passengers were returning home, and others, in transit, were setting off to discover the picturesque parts of the city. Young local boys, stripped to the waist, were showing all sorts of colorful objects to amused potential customers.

In my cabin, my roommate said in a barely audible, low-pitched voice, "Rest. You're better, but you've been weakened by what you've been through."

I thanked him for looking after me. He nodded. "By the way," he said, "I speak with difficulty. Don't take it personally."

He is sick, I said to myself. You could see it in his face. "Tell me about yourself," he said.

I wondered if I should tell him about Blanca, about our love, so happy and yet so foolishly complex. Instead, I said something else. "I'm a student. I'm going to the Far East because I'm preparing a doctoral dissertation on heresy in mysticism."

I also told him about the legend of the lost Jewish kingdom. It aroused his interest.

"What I'm intrigued by," he said, "is the oblivion. No one remembers this story."

"Well, we share an interest in the quest for hidden things," I said. "You might well ask: In order to probe his own abyss, does man have to detach himself from it? I would answer that sometimes we want to break the mirror by pushing back the horizons it contains."

He interrupted me. "And what if the mirror reflected the truth of the other within yourself? Wouldn't that be dangerous?"

I answered, "It would be a defeat. And I seek in mysticism a way to avoid it by plunging right in with eyes wide open."

Our conversation continued on various subjects: literature and its challenges, the reasoning of philosophers, the traps of youth and the despairing wisdom of old age. He spoke about everything except his life. Why? I dared to ask him the question. He answered after a long silence.

"One day in my peregrinations, I met an old man who claimed to return from faraway times. Wasted, with a fiery gaze and a head held high, he told me atrocious stories, sometimes very old and obscure, as if he had been implicated in them. Like this meeting, for instance: 'His name is Isaac, son of Abraham. As in the Bible. Both came close to the altar. But in his story, it was Isaac, the son, who came back alone. It was he who had the leading part. He said he was ready to reveal the truth known only to the Creator. But he warned me: Whoever would listen to his words would be condemned to go around with an inexpressible inner sadness that would never leave him, not even after his death.' "

I felt a chill.

A few days later, before arriving in Bombay, he said to me, "This is where I leave you. Perhaps someday we'll meet again. On the road, in an ashram or sanctuary. Don't be angry if I say nothing more. I don't have the right to. In one year and a day I'm going to take a vow of silence. Somewhere I hope to meet the man who knows the Messiah's name and identity as well as the date of his advent. When that happens, the whole world will know it, including you. On that day, man will understand that, faced with his destiny, which is his truth, questions and answers will have become one."

He handed me a thick envelope with a message written on it: "To be opened only in a year, three months and three nights." He asked me to give him my word. I did.

He had more than one name, but the ones he gave me were G'dalya and Paritus ben Pinhas ha-Cohen.

I never saw him again.

I often think back on our meeting and our conversations. But I never heard G'dalya mentioned again until I had returned to Europe with Blanca and several friends for a "pilgrimage to the roots," a popular trend at the time, especially among young Jews and Christians who had discovered the horrors of contemporary history. We were in Kraków—in other words, not far from the cursed place called "the black hole of History," where my father and Arele had been subjected to absolute evil. Young musicians entertained tourists in public places and on café terraces by singing and playing popular Jewish tunes from before the Upheaval. Blanca and our friends, worn out from the trip, had gone back to the hotel. I felt the need to take a walk in the evening air.

My gaze was attracted by a group of musicians who were forming a circle around a young and skinny bearded violinist who, with a look of concentration, was feigning to be playing: He was bowing vigorously and rhythmically, but his instrument had no strings.

During a pause I went up to him and offered him a drink. I spoke French, then English. He looked at me without understanding. "I don't speak Polish." When I tried Yiddish, we could converse. He wanted a glass of water. He said he was from "not very far away." He wanted me to call him simply "the musician." He was the only Jew in his group. I asked what he did when he wasn't playing. All sorts of things, he said. He listened to the rustling of trees in the wind and, around here, to the song of the dead buried beneath mountains of ash. He had been in Kraków only since the previous day, yet forever: Time was important to him only as the rhythm of a musical melody. I told him that I had played the violin as an adolescent, that I loved popular Hasidic tunes, which induced tears, smiles and fervor, and a joy arousing ecstasy. I asked about his way of "playing." "It's the violin," he replied. "I belong to it, whereas the other violins belong to the musicians." He had found his violin in a gutted Jewish house in the Carpathian Mountains. "When I bent over to dust it," the musician said, "it started to talk to me with a human voice, without trickery or stratagems. It begged to be taken away, to be cared for and loved by me; it couldn't bear living alone anymore, rejected by all. It was at the end of its tether, suffering too greatly. And when I hesitated, it promised to sing for me as no other instrument had ever sung. It would confide secrets to me that no other ears had ever heard. Its songs would give my happiness an age-old dimension; when

I was sad, it would change my sadness into a melody of such beauty and moving sonority that even the angels in heaven had never known anything like it. In short, it would become my faithful companion in both joy and anguish."

The musician of silence expressed himself with great seriousness—I would even say solemnity. I repressed my desire to smile. He had more to say, but he had to return to his group. The orchestra played until midnight. Though I was exhausted, I waited for the his return. Seeing how tired I was, he suggested meeting the following night.

The man fascinated me. I wanted to know who he really was. Whom had he learned such things from? Where did he live? I spent a sleepless night next to Blanca, wondering.

Rising at dawn, I walked alone around the small streets of the royal old city of Kraków, surrounded by ghosts coming down from the mountains, so close and so threatening. In the evening, with Blanca and our friends, I found the musician and his violin at the same place, shortly before he began "playing."

I asked him why his violin was silent.

"You really don't understand a thing," he replied in his calm, low voice. "My violin isn't silent. People just refuse to listen to it, so it resists them. But it expresses itself better than I do, better than all of us, and differently, it speaks. It speaks for all those who made use of it to express the meaning of their shattered lives. Composers, violinists, singers and dancers, all those who were moved, overwhelmed by love or hope, or sadness, changed by the curse of God and human misery, all those whose death throes live on in this instrument—this violin conveys their cries, their lamentations. But people are morally, mentally, humanly incapable of hearing it. I alone . . ."

He cut himself off.

"You alone what?"

"I was going to say, excuse me for being conceited, that I alone on this cursed earth am worthy of hearing it. But that's not true. I met someone else who was—an odd fellow, a wanderer, roaming in and out of other people's lives, he attended a solo concert I gave in France before a Hasidic audience. Why had so many people come out to hear a violinist whose violin produced no audible sound? Some out of curiosity. Some sought a very new or very old message, coming from the origins of history that plunge into the memory of God. Others saw it as an original work of poetry. One old man mentioned a Hasidic school that glorified silence. Another described a rabbinical marriage where he heard a whole orchestra made up of stringless violins. Oh, yes, the Hasidim are true romantics. In a large gathering, introducing twenty-odd great violinists (the orchestra accepts only good musicians), all with stringless violins, is a bold thing to do! And the audience, meditative and moved, listened to them. And every person heard them. I'm just a soloist, and I'm not sure that my listeners in France heard me. But what of it! I can hear my violin. And so did the other man.

"Tell me more about the other man."

"Yes, the odd fellow who looked like a happy beggar or an unhappy prince. He had just returned from India, Jerusalem and other places, from another era. He claimed he could understand things that elude understanding, see the invisible and triumph over the power of Death by removing its bare face. Our first encounter was stormy. I criticized him for hating the dead, whereas my violin tries to appease them. He replied that apparently I was too ignorant to understand the meaning of his approach: It was not the dead but Death that he wished to subdue. That's why he liked my violin and its music. He even offered to compose an oriental tune for my violin inspired by an ancient text taken from the Dead Sea Scrolls. I said in my view, my violin's sorrowful complaint was more closely connected to Christian Europe than to the Hebraic tradition. 'Good,' he replied. 'I'll find appropriate words in the New Testament or in Martin Luther. And if you dislike those, I also know some Bohemian tales.' This fellow, whom I met by chance in France, is a walking, living library—a kind of human miracle."

My heart began racing, as before a surprise. "How much time did you spend together?"

"Exactly a week."

Like me.

"Did he give you the song he promised?"

"He did. One without lyrics."

"And what was its message?"

"There was none. It's a song that tells all mankind: You don't deserve my words or my voice. In fact, you don't deserve our dreams or our lessons. Besides, you've never understood anything about our destiny."

I asked him to play the song on his stringless violin. He did. And I don't know why, but I began to sob tearlessly.

"It's the song of the murdered Hasidim, sung to thank their

ancestor, the Master of the Good Name, the Besht, for having inspired, guided and enriched them."

"So the fellow was a Hasid?"

"He was Hasid and anti-Hasid, a rationalist and a mystic, infinitely proud and deeply humble: He alone knows when the hour of Redemption will toll. But he won't tell anyone. Like my violin, he is silent."

I hesitatingly asked him the name of this mysterious person, fearful I'd be disappointed. I was not.

"He has several identities."

"But under which identity did he introduce himself to you?"

"G'dalya."

I knew it. I had guessed it from the beginning.

"He said he also went under the names Menahem, Yaakov and even One-Eyed Paritus. Yet he wasn't one-eyed. He saw people and things clearly. Why did he pretend to have only one eye? I don't know. But he understood the thirst of the gods and men's desire to make sparks fly, and also the language of birds and clouds."

I said I'd be very grateful if he could help me find this man.

"No problem," he said. "He comes here every evening to listen to my violin. He's among the crowd."

"How will I recognize him?" I didn't want to reveal that I had already met him once, at sea.

"Don't worry. He'll recognize you thanks to my instrument."

That evening, the musician played a Hasidic tune, which made me realize that, in the face of memory, joys and sorrows merge.

.   .   .

In his prison, in his turmoil, Shaltiel tells himself that he could use the musician right now, and especially this G'dalya who hides behind the figure of One-Eyed Paritus.

Suddenly he is panicked: He no longer remembers where he hid the envelope that G'dalya had given him.

Will he die without having spoken to him again?

Will he also die without an heir?

Like children, I was fond of old people. Their memories were my dreams. When you look at them, you never know if they're about to weep or sing. In my jail, I wondered if I would ever become an old man.

Old people walk slowly as though they are afraid of stumbling. Each step is a triumph. Every thought is a surprise. Every meeting is a new support, a whiff of hope.

There's nothing surprising about the fact that at a certain point in my career, I decided to devote myself to them. I wanted to acknowledge them, follow them, nourish them in my own way. I wanted to establish and share a bond with them, reassure them while collecting illuminated or dusty scraps of their stories. Thanks to my efforts, they will not be dispersed and scattered into the wind of oblivion. Perhaps one day in the near or distant future, there will be someone, still relatively young but bearing age-old memories, who will do for me what I tried to do for them.

The two abductors were separated most of the time. Ahmed was on duty during the day and Luigi at night. In the darkness, Shaltiel didn't always realize this. When he feared he would go mad, he thought of One-Eyed Paritus and his mystical madness. Shaltiel liked the Italian more than the Arab. Both were his enemies, his oppressors, his inquisitors, possibly even his executioners, but with one he could talk, while the other only heaped insults and threats on him. Before each conversation with the Italian, he would free Shaltiel's hands and offer him a glass of water.

Every cross-examination started with an exchange that was both simple and useless. But on this day it took an unexpected turn.

Shaltiel: How long are you going to keep me here?

Luigi: This isn't up to us. It's up to Israel and Washington.

Shaltiel: And if it were up to you, would you let me go?

Luigi shrugged.

Shaltiel: You're so different from your comrade. He loathes me. You don't.

Luigi: He's the one who has suffered in the flesh and whose heart was bruised. He was born in a Palestinian refugee camp. His father and grandfather are stateless and live on alms. They're humiliated constantly, from day to day, from month to month, from generation to generation. His elder brother was killed by an Israeli commando. His sister lost her fiancé; she hasn't stopped sobbing since. Have I said enough?

Shaltiel decided not to argue. But they started to discuss politics. Luigi said he was on the side of the Palestinians, in other words, of the Arabs, and therefore a staunch adversary of the Jewish state.

"I can understand," he said, "that the Jewish people, after centuries of suffering, needed a state, but why do the Palestinians have to pay the price?"

Chased from where they lived, asked Shaltiel, where could the desperate Jews go at the end of the Second World War?

"They could have gone home."

"Home? Poland? Hungary? Romania? Lithuania? Those who did return home were greeted with hostility and, in some places, with pogroms. You're Italian. Don't tell me you're a Holocaust denier. Are you aware of our history? We were almost annihilated in Europe. So many of the survivors in camps for displaced persons encountered closed doors in America and the Holy Land, and had only one alternative: to fulfill their ancestral dream and restore Jewish sovereignty in the Promised Land."

"You didn't answer my question: Even if the Jewish people deserved a homeland, why did it have to be Palestine?"

"Because no other people in the world have been as haunted as mine for thousands of years by the nostalgia of returning to the land of their ancestors."

"Nostalgia is a feeling that leaves me cold," Luigi said. "What I'm interested in is justice. I'm fighting so that justice is rendered to the oppressed Palestinians. You Jews have forgotten that your hope is founded on their despair."

This is still surreal, Shaltiel thought. Here I am in a basement, at the mercy of two killers. They want me to help them make their cause more attractive to the American Jewish community. They want me to share their condemnation of Israel. Since when have I become so important that my opinion has any effect on public opinion? And here I am defending Israel before the citizen of a country that had been allied with the country that had planned to exterminate my people. Am I dreaming?

I reminded Luigi of a few historical truths: There had never been a Palestinian state since the origins of Islam. It was only in 1947 that, for the first time, the concept of a legal and independent Arab state in Palestine appeared on a resolution adopted by the United Nations. This resolution, known as partition—between a Jewish state and an Arab state (not a Palestinian state)—had been accepted by Israel. The Arabs rejected it and chose violence instead. Had they accepted the partition plan, today Lydda and Jaffa would be part of a Palestinian state living peacefully alongside a smaller, if not weaker, Jewish state. And Ahmed could have grown up and led a peaceful, productive existence instead of devoting his days and nights to murder.

"All of this is past history," said Luigi in a flat voice. "Why go back in time? That was four generations ago. You can't blame the young people of today for the mistakes their grandparents made in 1947–48."

"Is it the fault of the Jews?" asked Shaltiel.

"And what about the Israeli occupation of the Palestinian territories? What do you say about that? Whose fault is that? And doesn't it remind you of anything?"

"You're Italian and cultured; you should be ashamed of yourself. How can you compare the sometimes harsh and severe attitude of Israeli soldiers on the West Bank with the atrocities of the Blackshirts and the SS in occupied Europe? The German occupation, do you know what it was like? What was involved? Torture by the Gestapo, roundups, the executions of hostages, absolute terror, the imprisonment of innocent people, ghettos, deportations to Auschwitz . . ."

"Stop talking," said Luigi, walking away.

They resumed their discussion the next day around the subject of terror.

"Do you know who I am?" asked Luigi. "I'm a revolutionary who repudiates people who refuse to understand my wounds. Molded by memory as well as by the rejection of memory, I live in history, aspiring to take part in its convulsions of love and hatred, in its lunacies. It is history that I condemn and history that judges me. I was trained by anarchists in Latin America, the Red Brigades in Italy and the Baader-Meinhof group in Germany. I'm a true internationalist. What unites us all is a faith in violence as the only way of influencing events."

Shaltiel remained silent.

"You have no comments to make about this? This doesn't shock you?"

"No. The world you live in is not mine. What do you know about mine or about me? All you know is that I'm at your mercy, and that when you hit me, it hurts."

"I never hit you."

"Your accomplice did, in your name too."

"That's not the same thing."

"In the world I live in, it's the same."

"Your world has failed. We're building ours on its ruins. I know our methods disgust you, but they work because of the fear we arouse. Fear is more tangible than promises. In the Middle Ages, people thought they could fight evil with evil. We want to fight fire with fire by increasing the scale and scope of the fire."

Shaltiel hesitated. Should he risk offending Luigi further? Quietly he said, "I'm sorry to have to tell you, but part of your argument is reminiscent of Hitler's Germany—Goebbels, Streicher, Eichmann, Mussolini. They all claimed they were waging a war against wars, bringing death to others in order to rescue their own people from death."

"So, as far as you're concerned, I'm a fascist, a Nazi! A monster, in other words!"

"I don't know you. But apart from their extreme nationalism, your logic is no less destructive than theirs."

The Italian managed to control his anger. "I'm not a Nazi or a racist. I don't advocate military conquest or domination; gratuitous cruelty repels me; death makes me ashamed. I'm only in favor of revolution."

"In other words, in favor of force."

"No, only in favor of violence."

"What kind of violence are you talking about that isn't cruel?"

"Stop!" said the Italian. "I'm not cruel. My Arab comrade is. Even more so than you could imagine. He fights for his own people; my struggle transcends that issue. If this event ends in your death, he will be the one responsible, not me."

Shaltiel drew a deep breath, though he felt a pain in his chest. Now it was clear: The last living examples of mankind that he would see in his lifetime would be his executioners.

And he'd die without an heir.

He sought Blanca in his hallucinations. He never ceased looking for her. Her hair verging on black, her refined face, her turned-up nose, her lips full of life, she was by his side even in his stifling hideaway. He heard her deep, low-pitched voice. He imagined her to be the ideal woman. It was best not to remember her faults. Her intransigence, her prying, her obstinacy: No one's perfect. Didn't Maimonides say that human beings should not aspire to perfection as God alone is the incarnation of perfection?

How could he explain their estrangement? Are love and staying power incompatible? Do human beings tire even of happiness? In the life of a couple, it can happen that one fine morning you wake up and the attraction is gone and you have nothing to say to each other anymore. There is no clash, no misunderstanding. It's just that the sacred flame is no longer sacred. There has been no betrayal, no extramarital relationship. We shut ourselves into words that we offer to the whole world, or rather to the small world that surrounds us and stifles us. The wife is as beautiful as ever and the husband no less devoted, and yet things have changed without any breakup having taken place. The Talmud is wise on the subject: "When a couple loves one another, they sleep well, even on the edge of a razor; as soon as love is gone, the largest bed seems too narrow." In the past, the sparks flew all the time.

It was odd for a man who loved children so much, who lived for them and for old people, that they had no children. Was it too late to think about it? Blanca wanted to have children, but Shaltiel did not. He quoted a passage in the Talmud for her, to the effect that at the time of the destruction of the Temple the Sages refused to marry because, they said, when God shows He intends to destroy the universe, it is forbidden to thwart His will by giving life.

He remembers their first meeting. He is twenty years old. A bohemian-artist type, nervous, extremely tense, fearful, always on the defensive. She is beautiful.

In their class at City College in New York, there are two hundred students listening to the lecture by the brilliant professor of moral philosophy Robert Goldmann, a campus celebrity. Shaltiel is in his third year, Blanca in her first. He is distracted as he listens to the lecture, while she, next to him, her head bent sideways, is taking notes like everyone else. He studies her profile, attracted by her way of concentrating and ignoring his presence. He does not conceal his attraction. She is the center of his thoughts. This has never happened to him before.

That day's Nietzsche lecture is about his years of dementia and silence. Was he a deep metaphysician or a flamboyant poet? The professor admires him for his style and his poetic originality. According to him, when Nietzsche first writes a verse or a thought, he has no idea where it will lead him. His knowledge is tragic, hardly gay. Zarathustra lets himself be carried along by the luminous force that, from the outset, eludes his darkened consciousness. Which proves that Nietzsche himself didn't want to be followed in his madness and even less in his suicide.

Is there such a thing as poetic, literary philosophy, philosophical literature? Didn't Bergson receive the Nobel Prize in Literature? Plato's dialogues lack style, élan, hence grace and beauty, but what does that prove?

Shaltiel doubts that the young student, with her dark hair, tilted head and bright eyes, feels his presence. But it is she who, without raising her head, addresses him first with a forced smile before he has said a word to her.

"I haven't seen you write anything down. You must have an exceptional memory."

Shaltiel is startled and says nothing.

"But," she goes on, her head still bent over her notebook.

"But what?"

"There are two possibilities: Either it's our professor or it's Nietzsche that you're not very interested in."

He stammers. "Both fascinate me."

"Yet I have the impression you're not listening."

"I'm listening while looking."

Her name is Blanca. She has not been in love yet with anyone—at least, that's what he thinks. They have coffee together. As Shaltiel dreads personal exchanges, he dwells on the subject that absorbs them in their course: Nietzsche. His romantic fate that can only leave people perplexed. His despair, his rebellions. And above all, his long solitary career, far from society and the academies. Did he have a disturbance of the mind? Did he lack inspiration? Had he simply lost his bearings?

Blanca doesn't want to study pure philosophy but philosophy of art. For her, Michelangelo and Goya, Brueghel and Soutine, are not just great painters, but also genuine thinkers. They put ideas into their works as well as form. The genius of the great medieval artists who dealt with religious subject matter was that though they painted at the request of patrons, as they worked on their canvases they perceived the true meaning of life and Creation. In his sketches of the Sacrifice of Isaac, doesn't the message that Rembrandt introduces reflect his longing to understand the eternal question of the relationship between the Creator and His creations, hence between Father and Son? The ancients were right: The philosopher's quest prevails over the quest of all the sciences.

Perhaps because of the biblical reference, Shaltiel wonders if she is Jewish. How can he ask her without offending her, without looking ridiculous? But he needs to know. He cannot forget where he comes from.

He need only conjure the image of his elderly, stooped father, with his haunted gaze, to remember. He wouldn't want to hurt him for anything in the world. To add sorrow to his pain. It would be unthinkable, unpardonable. It is why Shaltiel has never dated a young girl.

But what should he do now? He chooses to wait. Next time, he will find a way of bringing up the subject in the course of the conversation. It turns out she is Jewish and an only daughter. Her parents had left Germany for the United States in 1933. They were observant but only moderately so; faithful to tradition, but actively anti-fundamentalist. The father is a renowned lawyer; the mother, a respected art critic. Both are influential, card-carrying Democrats.

Like Shaltiel, but for different reasons, Blanca wants to understand evil. It's their first feeling of deep mutual understanding. There is their first kiss, overwhelming warmth, the awakening of desire. They make discoveries together.

At first, they see each other only twice a week at the university. Afterward, they also meet in Central Park. They go to the theater and the movies. But Shaltiel still blushes each time she takes his hand or charms him with her captivating smile. One May evening, sitting on a bench in the verdant park, they exchange stories of their families, so different from one another. What do the memories of Weimar Germany have in common with those of Eastern Europe in its darkest days?

"At home," Blanca says, "my parents sometimes speak in German so I won't understand them."

"Mine speak Yiddish, probably out of habit. Except that I adore the language, for its warmth and flavor. There are some Yiddish words that remain untranslatable: '*Rakhmoness*' is different than 'pity.' '*Hak mir nisht a chénik,*' 'cut me a teapot,' doesn't have the same meaning as 'leave me alone.' "

"In German," says Blanca, "which is close to Yiddish, sentences are often long, heavy, solemn. Everything seems so serious, not to say menacing at times. Perhaps because to us it is linked to such atrocities."

They talk about the secrets, the silences of their families. Shaltiel's parents hardly talk about their experiences—they are too painful—whereas Blanca's parents recall theirs with nostalgia and all too often. What do they know of the secrets that their children carry within them?

Suddenly, Shaltiel's jailers stopped resorting to torture, and even to violence, except verbally. They removed his blindfold and untied his stiffened arms. He had to force his eyelids open.

His first reaction on recovering his sight was a jolt of panic: What was happening was so unexpected that it must have a dire explanation. Now he could clearly see his two jailers. They were no longer wearing masks. This could only mean that the end was approaching. His captors were talking in the corner of the room. As always, at moments like this that he called "crossroads in time," to avoid thinking about the inevitable, he conjured up the wrinkled face of old One-Eyed Paritus.

Tell me, dear Paritus, he said to himself, were you ever tortured because you were innocent? Were you ever so close to your impending death? Were you ever imprisoned? You used to tell me that sometimes man is his own prisoner. But for the free man could prison be a mere transition? And his liberation, even partial, a transformation? What will I do with the stories, mine and yours, that are buzzing in my head, in a thunderous, dark chaos streaked with lightning?

He tried to take a good look at the two men who were facing him. One tall, the other short; the visionary and the brute. The Arab was talking animatedly; Luigi was listening intently. Rubbing his hands to get his blood circulating, Shaltiel waited.

"You filthy Yid, you lied to us," yelled the Arab, gesticulating as the two men approached him. "By saying the truth, you got us thinking you were lying. For you, truth and lies are intertwined. If our Prophet were alive, he would strangle you with his own holy hands. Now we know you're not an important person; you don't matter to anyone, except to your family, and no one is interested in them. You write and no one reads you; you talk and no one listens. Your life, just like your faith, doesn't carry weight with anyone. We're the only people to take you seriously, that's the truth. From now on, we're all three interconnected."

Shaltiel remained silent. He had no answer. The Arab went on.

"Now we know that your confession, even if sincere, doesn't count for much. It's worthless to your people, and to us too."

Shaltiel understood nothing in this verbal avalanche with its perverse logic. What was his torturer talking about?

"If I understand you correctly, you've tortured me for nothing. You've deprived me of sleep, food, rest and even hope—for nothing," said Shaltiel. "You made me go through a hellish agony for nothing. You humiliated me for nothing. And what about my family? Have you thought about my relatives who must be suffering from anxiety and pain? By what right do you torture them? My elderly parents and my wife? You hurt people, you make them suffer, and you don't even know what purpose it serves? Didn't you just admit that it was all for nothing?"

"For nothing, you say, you lousy Jewish bastard? We're not done with you yet—with you or your kin. And it might turn to out to be worse than death."

Forgetting the sharp, throbbing pain in his body, Shaltiel cried out, "What are you going to do to me?"

"Just shut up!"

The Arab whispered a few words to his accomplice and left the basement with a look of disgust.

Left alone with Luigi, who had been silent throughout, Shaltiel focused his gaze on the man who was scrutinizing him intently, hands clasped, with curiosity but no hatred. What is his function in this situation, which is as absurd as it is atrocious?

"A German journal that is close to our cause reprinted your entertaining article on the dreams of a madman. Your piece is a fantasy and not a confession. I'm not surprised that it had no success with the public. And for me, a revolutionary, this flight into the unreal makes no sense. Believe me, I'm sincerely sorry about the ordeal we've put you through. But for the revolution to triumph, it must never fear mistakes, slipups . . . We know how to turn the page quickly, very quickly."

He continued to hold forth while Shaltiel gradually discovered the area that surrounded him.

"In the beginning, of course, we chose you by chance," Luigi explained. "But everything that happened afterward was because of your damn article. We took it seriously. What can I say? We thought your text had political weight for your readers and that we could take advantage of it. It's the general rule for those of us who like revolutions. We take everything seriously, the innocuous as well as the essential. Life and death. As a tool, death still has no equal."

This man is insane, Shaltiel said to himself. The other one is insane with hatred and this one is insanely ambitious.

"In principle, you were supposed to be our prisoner of war. That was our idea initially. Now we realize we made a mistake. But it makes no difference as far as you're concerned. You're our prisoner; your life or your death can help the revolution."

"And you're considering my execution as a possibility," said Shaltiel, trying to control his fear and despair. "The two of you are probably going to murder me in the name of a ludicrous ideology, right?"

"Yes," replied the Italian in a sober voice. "We might have to eliminate you. You have to understand, Mr. Feigenberg: The revolution requires a state of permanent warfare. Whoever is not with us is against us. Whoever rises up against our Palestinian allies is our enemy."

"And this enemy, irrespective of who he is, you're just going to kill him? Is that the rule of the game?"

"The revolution isn't a game. It has its own justice, its own conception of justice, its own conception of life and death, and especially of history, yes, history, its impulses, its rough sketches, its challenges. In a world in which the enemy has quasi-unlimited powers, we have to be more violent, more radical, definitive in wielding ours. As every revolutionary is prepared to sacrifice his own life for an ideal, why should he refrain from sacrificing the life of his enemy?"

Shaltiel was too exhausted to think of a pertinent response. His interlocutor was in his forties, taciturn, wearing a gray suit, black tie and orange shirt. He had something of an outsider or a deposed aristocrat in his nonchalance. He was intelligent, cultured, even sensitive at times. Most probably he too had a family. Maybe he still had his parents. Did he think about them as much as Shaltiel thought about his relatives? How did he come to be standing in front of me? What's his story? Coughing softly, he appealed to his jailer.

"You speak to me about power and revolution, but I don't understand a thing about them. They're out of my range. I have no feelings either way. I live my life on the sidelines. I want my approach to be humble; my dreams don't stand out—they're simple and straightforward. Apparently you're already aware of this: I'm not important or in any way influential. I'm just a storyteller, a writer, nothing more, nothing else. My life has value only for my relatives. They must be dreadfully worried about me. So let me go back to them. And for you, the page will be turned."

While he was speaking, Shaltiel studied the enemy standing before him. He was disquieted. His behavior revealed a vague doubt. Was he looking for a response to his own destiny in his prisoner and possible victim? He was a better listener than his accomplice. In some strange way, Shaltiel imagined for an instant that this man could one day be his savior.

"Listen to me closely, Mr. Storyteller," said Luigi. "Life isn't a tale. And man has better things to do with the years in his life than lull himself to sleep with twaddle. Our goal is our duty: to change the beliefs and habits of the masses, and change the attitude of their leaders so that freedom will be given to those who are deprived of it and happiness to those who wake up every morning in misfortune. Am I expressing myself clearly enough?"

"You're referring to the Arabs?"

"In this instance, yes. For us, they're like the proletariat in Lenin's time. The Jews are their oppressors; that's why we're fighting against them."

Shaltiel was in danger of death, and here he was discussing the meaning of truth in history with someone who had no qualms being an executioner.

"I'm not a political activist, sir," said Shaltiel, "but I have studied history. What are the secret forces that shape it? I try to work it out. The Jewish people, in exile for two thousand years, never oppressed another people, never humiliated a person for his religion, skin color, ethnicity or social affiliation. We never demanded dignity for ourselves at the expense of others. We have been victims too long to want to become the executioners of those who dream of living happily and in peace."

"You're forgetting one simple thing," said his captor. "You've always lived to make us feel guilty. Christians, progressives, Europeans, their allies—this is the impression you've always conveyed. You accuse us of not having done enough for you. It's as if history had invented you for this sole exercise: to judge us. And you want us to love you? The enlightened, civilized world that believes in the future of humanity says this to you: It's had enough! Enough of you and your lessons, enough of your complaints and recriminations, enough of your wanting to live and survive in a society that doesn't want you. Your problem is that you've learned nothing from your own history."

When you're choking with anger and rage, One-Eyed Paritus had once said to Shaltiel, try not to show it. Remember, the loudest cry is the one you don't utter. He made an effort to force his voice to be calm and answered: "In other words, if I understand you correctly, sir, you'd like to see all of us vanish from the face of the earth and then you'd show us respect, affection and gratitude. That's the meaning of your remarks and your conclusion? Well, you should know that others before you have tried to exclude us, diminish us and wipe us out using this method. The most recent such person was Adolf Hitler."

"That was then; this is now," said the Italian, eliding the argument. "The man who now holds your fate in his hands is a Muslim. And I believe in the benefits of the Revolution."

Shaltiel thought that if he came out of this alive, he would go visit the old men who lived and worked, each in his own way, for revolutionary ideals. His story might entertain them. And if he was murdered, he would have a very special story to relate to the heavenly court.

Ahmed had become melancholic. It was as if he had suffered some kind of attack. Things were not going according to plan, and it was affecting him.

"I sometimes say to myself," he said to Luigi, "that I've

ruined my life. I miss my family. My wife. My children. I see them when I open my eyes at dawn. They smile at me. I tell them that they'll be proud of their father one day as I am of them. I know they're dead, but their smile makes them come back to life. I don't see them in my dreams. When they were alive, I used to dream about them. My dreams have changed. They are haunted by my enemies. I kill them in my dreams. They've replaced my loved ones. My loathing for the infidels throws a shadow over the love I had for each member of my family. Initially, as a young soldier for the Prophet, I saw myself rising to seventh heaven. During the training period in the desert, we would dance around the fire in the evening singing of our faith. Thanks to us and our sacrifices, I will no longer be uprooted, stateless, an exile everywhere in the West. Along with my comrades, we'll build the future of our nation in a violent kingdom, purified by violence. For the first time in history, there will be a Palestinian state, free and proud. Meanwhile, here I am with you in this dungeon, facing a man who refuses to give in. If someone had told us that the strength of this storyteller would be greater than ours, would you have believed him?"

"Yes," answered Luigi.

"That doesn't bother you?"

"No. It doesn't."

"That's because you're Italian."

"That's true. We like stories."

"So do we," said Ahmed. "But we don't like all storytellers. Not this one, for example."

Hearing Ahmed express his doubts, Shaltiel had the crazy thought to appeal to them man to man.

"Listen to me," he said, surprised by the sound of his own voice. They didn't hear him. "Listen to me," he repeated.

This time, they heard him. Ahmed walked over and stood in front of him.

"What do you want, you dirty Jew?" Ahmed cried out, ready to hit him.

"I'd like to tell you something."

"A Jewish tale? Another one? This is what I think of your tales."

He struck him in the face.

"Leave him alone," Luigi said. He looked at Shaltiel. "We're listening."

"This is a poem that is supposed to be a prayer or a vision," he said in a voice that he hoped was strong and deep. "It's not by me, but by an old immortal Sage. He ascribed it to a mute Etruscan.

Here is what
the condemned man,
in his prison,
wishes to offer as a gift.
Morning wind,
midnight shadows:
carry away my calls
to joy, to life.
Black tears,
sunlit dreams:
be my witnesses
silent and immortal.

The wandering child,
the lost ascetic:
it's me they question,
it's me who looks for them.
I call for you, men;
I love you, women:
my soul begs for you;
and my body too.
God, where are you?
Lord: Where are we?
With you, everything is possible;
but far away.
Without you, nothing is close,
but with you, you are far.
So very far.
In your own prison.

"I like the Etruscans," said Luigi.

"Why?" asked Ahmed.

"Because they were all massacred and yet they continue to give us poems."

"I don't understand them," said Ahmed.

"I don't either," said Luigi, "but I like them."

Later on, alone in the musty-smelling basement, Shaltiel wondered: Didn't he live in the Tower of Babel? Didn't we all? In those days, languages were all mixed together, words had no more meaning, people didn't understand their fellow men. My listeners, what are their languages? My torturers, what is their true language? What's the point of making words to tell the truth about life if no one listens to you or understands you?

The storyteller and his ramblings. Locked up in a jail built of words.

In school, Shaltiel remembered, no one knew anything about the situation and destiny of his strange schoolmate, Yohanan. The handsome adolescent was different from the others. He was withdrawn, timid, detached from his environment; he never raised his voice but listened intently to everything that was being said. Sometimes he uttered incoherent sounds, unintelligible noises whose meaning no one understood. Amused or serious, he seemed to be attuned to a different universe. Some students made fun of him at first. Admonished by their teacher, they stopped. He had been accepted into the school out of compassion for his parents or grandparents, who had greatly suffered in exile, it was said.

One day, he stopped coming to class. It was thought that his parents had taken him on a trip or placed him in a specialized institution. Later, Shaltiel learned the details. The world-renowned ethnologist Professor Robert Marcus was a friend of Yohanan's father. He came to visit him one evening and, by chance, he heard the boy's babbling. "He's ill," his father said. Intrigued, Dr. Marcus listened to him attentively. The noises followed a regular rhythm. It took a trained ear to hear them. "Your son isn't ill," he said to his friend. The scientist returned to the house regularly. He and Yohanan became inseparable. Ten months later, an international academic colloquium was held in New York where about twenty ethnologists were invited to listen to Yohanan. Guided and supported by Dr. Marcus, the young adolescent recalled distant events in his language. Specialized journals devoted enthusiastic pages to him. One of Marcus's students chose him as the subject of his doctoral thesis.

One morning, to everyone's astonishment, he started to pronounce a few simple words: He was hungry and thirsty. He said he missed someone who was waiting for him. He died a short time later with a smile on his lips. Professor Marcus delivered the funeral oration. He said, "Beloved Yohanan, you knew a truth that is hidden from us, that of the ancients, and now you brought it back to them, intact and pure."

"Yohanan's poem," Shaltiel said, "is a prayer. Sometimes it is recited by man, at other times by God himself. Both are in jail."

"I like it," said Luigi. "Your friend makes me sad, but I like that sadness."

And what if I myself were Yohanan? Shaltiel wondered. And what if my present-day stories were addressed to generations buried centuries ago? And who will relate—and in what language—the story I am living through right now?

I was unaware that initially my two jailers belonged to two different small groups but later joined a large terrorist movement recently founded in America by a young Saudi activist known as Hassan ibn Hassan. Their strategy was to destabilize the situation in Israel by striking American Jews, Israel's main supporters. That's how, by pure chance, I became their target. It was the Mossad envoy who first suggested the possibility. It was soon confirmed by a message received at *The New York Times*.

Below is its content, similar to the message Blanca had received at the beginning of this misadventure.

> To whom it may concern: We are detaining the Jewish writer Shaltiel Feigenberg. He is our hostage. If they wish to see him again alive, the Jewish authorities in Tel Aviv and Washington will have to free three of our people who are in prison for their heroic combat against the occupation of their land. Today the prisoner is in good health. But his future is no longer in our hands.

That evening Luigi revealed to me the terms of the deal.

"There's still a chance you'll survive," he said. "We're waiting for the official response to our request. I'm confident."

"What accounts for your confidence?"

"The pity I have for you."

"The pity for what?"

"We thought you were someone else; it's silly, but that's what happened. We made you suffer without even thinking about who you were."

"Should I thank you for your humane confession? Have no illusions: Your deal won't be accepted by either America or Israel. They'll see it as despicable and they'll be right."

"In that case, be aware that you'll never see your family again."

Later, my thoughts turned to my older brother, Pavel. Hadn't he gone to Moscow to help the revolution?

So I'll die soon. That's obvious. Terror, that refined prison of modern times, imposes its law—*a* implies *b*. It was clear from the first day, the first hour. The Arab's voice said it clearly, regardless of his words.

At this fateful moment facing death, does everyone, the patient in the hospital, the exhausted old man, have the same feeling, not of incoherence but of confusion? Does thought move forward or backward in fits and starts? Does the rhythm of time slow and gather speed independently of our will? Does childhood become close and the future distant and inaccessible? For me, the planet has shrunken to the size of a basement. I see now that I will live out the rest of my days with these two enemies as my sole companions. They alone will be present for my last minutes on earth. It will be their images that I'll bring with me into the other world. But to whom will I relate the story of my final hours?

Now everything will depend on the downhill speed.

In prison, you cling to memory. It's a form of freedom.

I am about five or six years old. It's a summer day. The sky and everything else is luminous: the face of my grandfather as he takes me into his garden, the grass, the fruit trees. I pick up a plum. I recite the appropriate prayer before putting it in my mouth. My grandfather congratulates me. "That's good, my child. Do you know who eats without praying?" I don't know. He tells me. "Animals. They eat because they're hungry."

I answer, "And I ate that plum without being hungry."

"It's true. You ate that plum because it was there."

"But why the prayer? In order to thank God?" I say.

"Yes, that's it. To thank God, blessed be He." Grandfather nods his head and asks me to translate the prayer:

"Blessed are You, God, our God, King of the universe, who has created the fruit of the tree."

My grandfather smiles. "But the words 'thank you' aren't included! You're just blessing God." I probably disappointed my grandfather. He caresses my head and says, "Every prayer means acknowledging that everything on man's earth comes from the Creator: the leaves rustling in the wind, wine, thirst, the clouds and the sun, joys and sorrows, happiness and desire—as well as this moment in time that we're spending together."

He kisses me on the forehead. And we continue our walk. I love my grandfather. He has been dead for years, but I love him in the present. Tall, majestic, his eyes alternately feverish and soothing. He is there when I call him. Did I sometimes call out to him without knowing why? Just to hear his voice? To make sure he could hear me?

But now, I don't understand: What's this incident doing in my prison? Oh yes, I remember. My grandfather concluded in a whisper: "You're at the bottom of the mountain. May you climb up without suffering."

From my father, I heard spellbinding stories about my grandfather. He raised his children in a small village next to his native town. He owned an inn and his whole family worked in it. It was closed on Saturdays, which complicated matters for Christian customers. Most of them understood. However, every so often drunkards came and knocked at the door, demanding a bottle on the Sabbath. Some of them threatened to wreck the place. My courageous grandfather confronted them in his Sabbath clothes and told them in no uncertain terms that the God of the Jews could strike them dead in the blink of an eye. The hotheads always backed off, except once when there was a brawl. Grandfather and his children lost one battle, but not their honor.

Help, Grandfather!

I miss being able to wash. I feel dirty, ugly, disgusting. The bathroom is nearby, and when I hear the water running, that too tortures me. I'm tied to a stool now; before I was spread out on the floor. My wrists and ankles are sore. The migraines continue. It takes an intense mental effort to summon those I love, living and dead.

Memory, please stay open for the beloved faces, the smiles, joys, words of my father. My love for them makes me vulnerable, fragile. I will die far away from them.

The door opens quietly. My abductors are both there. No doubt they're bringing me my meal: stale bread and lukewarm water, as usual? Is it my morning meal or evening meal? I'm more thirsty than hungry. They've released my wrists so I can go to the toilet, but they still hurt. So do my eyes. The men help me climb to the first floor. In a dry, hoarse voice, the Arab says to me, "Look around. You feel the air? We opened the window a bit, so you can see the world you're about to leave. Look at the apple tree; take it in. It's the last one you'll see. And don't blame us for all of this. Blame your Jews. They're still rejecting our conditions. Meanwhile, you're being of no help to us. We just want you to write a letter begging them to have pity on you and your family. And to free the three prisoners."

My heart is pounding so hard I'm afraid it could burst.

God of my forefathers, protect those who love me and whom I love.

We're in the synagogue. It's packed for Yom Kippur. My grandfather explains the prayers to me. God, the King of Kings, sits on His throne on high and judges the living: who will live and who will die; who will be brought down and who will be elevated. I ask, "Does He also judge the judges who have imprisoned so many Jews, Papa?" His finger on his lips, he lets me know that it is forbidden to talk during the solemn prayer. Afterward, he tells me, "God, blessed be He, is just; He is the source of all truths; His truth is the reward of good people and the punishment of the impious."

Why this memory? What is truth doing in this cursed place, right now, on what is surely the last day of my life?

My father later told me how this litany had been composed and by whom. This is the medieval story of Rabbi Amnon of Mainz. It was three days before the New Year. When the local bishop ordered the Jewish inhabitants to convert to Christianity, the great scholar requested three days of reflection, which he regretted with all his heart. He should have said no right away. He was tortured, his limbs amputated. Upon his request, he was carried into the synagogue, where the congregation was praying, observing the rites of Rosh Hashanah. He asked that the service be interrupted and, with his last breath, recited the prayer I just mentioned. What about me? What will I do with my last breath?

Later in the service, there is mention of the ten martyrs who were executed for their loyalty to the faith. They were summoned before the tyrannical emperor Hadrian, who questioned them: "What does the Jewish Law say about a person who abducts one of his fellow men in order to sell him into slavery?"

"The law would have him sentenced to death," they say. "Freedom is no less important than life."

"But weren't your ancestors, the sons of Jacob, guilty of this crime when they sold Joseph into slavery? You shall be punished instead of them."

Suddenly I understand why all these memories come to mind: so that I'll think about my predicament as a hostage. Does it come up in the Bible or the Talmud? What misdeeds, and whose misdeeds, am I expiating? Could it be that I involuntarily offended, upset, hurt and put someone in danger?

Ahmed is very annoyed.

"Your Jewish friends here and in Israel are abandoning you. If you're honest with yourself, you must take a stand against their cruelty to you. And, at the same time, against the atrocities of the Jewish occupation of Palestine."

"No. I'm an American Jew tied to Israel by my soul. You can hit my body, you can wound it and even destroy it, but my soul will remain free, outside your reach. You'll never imprison it."

I don't consider myself a hero. I never have been one. I live from the fruits of my imagination and memory. Storyteller, writer, that's my profession. Words are my only possession. I entertain children on their birthdays. Sometimes I fulfill the duties of cantor at religious Jewish marriages. And here I am being tormented as if I were a courageous spy, the author of heroic exploits.

"Your soul, you dare speak of your soul! You're Jewish, and Jews have no soul! The enemies of Islam have no soul!"

"I'm not an enemy of Islam."

"All Yids are."

"I'm Jewish, but I've never been an enemy of other religions. I don't know how one becomes one."

"You could at least admit you're loyal to the Jewish state that despoils Arab lands! And you won't sign a letter to your Jewish friends demanding they put pressure on the governments concerned?"

"No, I won't sign anything."

The Arab strikes me on my head, on the back of my neck, in my stomach. The Italian says and does nothing. Motionless, he stares at me fixedly and lets his comrade get his hands dirty. I hear myself moan and this humiliates me.

"You loathe us," the Arab yells. "Your loathing makes you proud. But it will also make you sorry you came out of your mother's belly."

Why does the Arab speak of pride? Because I love Israel,

and my passion for Jerusalem has never died? If praying for David's eternal city is an act of war, then, yes, I'm guilty. But not of anything else.

The Arab torturer pulls me out of my reverie brutally.

"Here's something you wrote . . ."

He brings a sheet of paper up to my bloodied face. I can't see well. It's a newspaper clipping through the narrow slit. My torturer starts to read passages from the newspaper. He slaps me in the face systematically after each sentence. I pass out.

When I awake, I see my grandfather, with his soft white beard. He urges me not to cry; it's too painful for him when I cry. Nor can God on high bear the tears of a good little Jewish boy crying. He knows I like stories, so he tells me one.

One day, the illustrious Hasidic Master, Rabbi Israel Baal Shem Tov, gathers his closest disciples in secrecy to teach them the mysteries of the final Redemption: how and when to recite certain litanies; say the number for each of the heavenly angels; take the ritual bath and cite specific verses of the Psalms and the Zohar; practice an absolute asceticism of silence and chastity for a specific number of days and nights. All the things that had come down to him from his Masters—and to them from theirs, going back to Rabbi Hayim Vital and the Ari, and as far back as Moses, all the things concerning the advent of the Messiah—he passed on to them. And he arranged for the next meeting to be at the edge of the forest. Together, they would strike up a sad song and, thanks to their fervor and mystical power, it would change into a triumphal hymn that could reverse the course of history, and the Messiah would see the Jewish people suffering in exile, and all of humanity, ill and severely wounded. Then, in an immense movement of compassion, he would announce the end of the wait.

Well, said my grandfather after a sigh, the Master and his disciples went home separately and, loyal to their common wish, they each followed the instructions to the letter.

The special day arrived. All the disciples, in ecstasy, met at the designated place in the forest. They waited for their Master, who was late. Agonizing hours went by. Finally, he appeared, exhausted, and more melancholic than ever. Do you know what he said to them? my grandfather asked me. "I'm proud of you, my young companions," said the Master, "proud of being your link to your great ancestors, proud of having helped you move closer to the one who still has the mission of saving our people from despair and healing humanity of its illnesses. He was very near tonight. Everything was made ready for the unique moment. You were waiting for him and he was waiting for you. Yes, the Messiah too was waiting for the meeting. But on my way here, a few steps before reaching you, I heard a child cry in a hut near the edge of the forest. His cries were heartbreaking. His mother had probably gone to fetch wood for the hearth, or milk. So, brothers and friends, I couldn't help opening the door to the hut, stepping inside, looking at the baby in his shabby cradle, singing a lullaby for him and consoling him. Do you understand? When a child cries like this, the Messiah can and must wait."

And I, in the arms of my grandfather, cried, but he knew it was out of love.

Was it the third day or the thirtieth? Like any man doomed to despair, Shaltiel has lost all sense of time. Ever since his blindfold was removed, he knows where he is and why, but he doesn't know how long death will wait before snatching him away from the living. Oddly, he wishes he could look at himself in the mirror. Has his beard turned white? Does he look like his grandfather? He notices that the lamp hanging from the sooty ceiling is swaying. Will it crash to the floor with a deafening noise that could alert a vigilant pedestrian in the street?

The Italian speaks to him gently. He's cajoling.

"Don't blame us. You're really a victim of chance, not of us. You happened to be crossing our path at the wrong time. We had to take someone hostage. It could have been some other stranger, some other passerby. A young Protestant or an elderly Catholic. If you'd stayed at the library another hour, or at home, you would be with your family right now, listening to the news on television. A charming anchorwoman would be announcing the latest bulletin: Terrorists have just abducted . . . someone else. You'd be getting clever analyses from pundits. So far, the police are unable to determine whether this is a political act or a criminal one. Oh, if only you had taken a taxi home. You know, I find you kind of likable, my friend."

"You're my torturer and I'm your prisoner. Will these always be our roles? I didn't choose my role."

"I did," says Luigi, after a pause.

Shaltiel realizes the absurdity of the situation. He's going to die, and here he is, taking an interest in his enemy's inner life.

"Did you really decide to hurt me, to torture me? I don't believe you."

"Yet it's the truth."

"So, explain it to me . . . before performing your 'duty,' " says Shaltiel, trying, unsuccessfully, to smile. "If I understand you correctly, you'll accomplish this duty even if you're loath to do so? Or am I wrong?"

"No, you're not. You call me a torturer, an executioner, a murderer, and God knows what else, whereas I say I'm a revolutionary."

"And this allows you to torture and kill human beings?"

"Didn't you study the history of nations and mankind? The end justifies the means."

"All means?"

"Yes. All means."

"Are you sure that history demands this? What gives you the right to speak in its name?"

"Being a revolutionary means making a claim to this right, and obtaining it by having an effect and influencing history."

"In other words, by submitting history to your own will, by making it your slave, though you say you want to free it. You say you're obeying it, whereas, in the name of your theories, you're trying to eliminate it and substitute your own. But, admit it, your theories are not very pretty, for they lead to the ugliness of extreme violence that is the negation of life."

Shaltiel summons all of his intellectual and physical powers in order to engage in this impossible debate, as if to proclaim that the torture wracking his body is an abstraction. Is there an example of an SS officer discussing his role of killer with his victim? Can murderers and executioners define themselves and make distinctions among themselves, under the pretext that they are acting in the name of different principles and obeying rules that have nothing in common, other than the shedding of blood of innocent people? Can one wonder about the place of innocence in the revolutionary venture? And what if the latter draws its strength from the very fact that it condemns the innocence of its victims more than their supposed guilt? And what if, ultimately, what is called revolution was merely a reflection of evil in the whole gamut of theories invented by men who use their power to dehumanize history?

"What am I to you?" Shaltiel asks. "A prisoner? A hostage? Just one more victim? A Jew? A human being?"

"All of these, perhaps."

"How will my suffering and the suffering of my family advance your struggle?"

"Thanks to you, little storyteller, our enemies will take us more seriously."

"But you claim to be fighting for society's victims. Well, what about me? Aren't I a victim too? More real, more palpable, more concrete than the others, who are far away and whom you've only seen on television screens or magazine covers?"

"There you're mistaken. I've traveled to refugee camps in Asia, starving populations in Africa. People who are exploited everywhere in the West. I'm fighting for them as well."

"But why choose terror, when there are other more honorable ways of coming to their aid? Did you give this any thought?"

"Yes, I did. But all those aid agencies, all those philanthropic organizations, are founded and manipulated by corporations that are responsible for the poverty and shameful conditions of the suffering victims. Not the revolution."

"But it brings about its own injustices. Am I not a living example—I mean, a still living example? Isn't communism a revolution that betrayed its own ideals? Didn't your Mussolini use the same arguments as you to impose his fascist dictatorship? Didn't Hitler shout that his mission was to help all of humanity?"

The lightbulb on the ceiling goes out. The basement is plunged into a kind of semidarkness. The Italian remains motionless and silent for a long time. Is he thinking about what he just heard or of what he will feel when this event reaches its epilogue? He seems less confident and gloomier when, for the first time, he answers in a more solemn voice.

"Your questions, or most of them, are not new to me. I've already weighed them in my mind, even though it was in other circumstances. What I'll say to you is what I said to myself, many years ago. There's no risk in admitting it to you: You'll take what you have the right to call my confession into the hereafter. And, who knows, there you might meet someone who will tell you what to do in a world that disowns us, a world that self-destructs by spreading death all over, that suffers by causing suffering, that chooses to ignore the meaning of its own cruelty and its consequences. These questions haunted me for a long time. My father was a despicable person. You should have suspected as much. Corrupt, pro-Mussolini and pro-Hitler, yes, fascist, Nazi. Seduced by the power and harshness of that ideology, he gave in to all its monstrous temptations. To put it plainly: He arranged to be assigned to very special SS units. I'm sure you know what I'm referring to, what kinds of people. I was born ten years later and was too young to understand his commitments and fully gauge how heinous they were. Why did he burden me with a past that I abhor and a fate that condemns me? He disgusted me. And being his son, living in his house, sharing his meals, just being alive, made me disgusted with myself too. I am living on the ruins of so many cultures destroyed by so many crimes; so many so-called noble and lofty passions producing so much rot. How could all of 'that' have happened? I wondered day and night. How could everything that was supposed to glorify truth have been swallowed up in a hideous, cruel and monstrous lie?"

Shaltiel is listening intently, resisting the slightest impulse to foolishly take pity on his torturer and possible executioner. He knows he needs to resist the Stockholm syndrome. He knows that in human relationships there are boundaries and that the Italian has crossed them all. Now, the Italian leaves the room.

Suddenly, Shaltiel conjures up Blanca again—her radiant and eager face when he tells her stories, her voice when she replies. One day, they went for a walk along the banks of a river. They both offered the river words as gifts. He said, "Return." She said, "Dream." Then he said, "Happiness." And she, "Always."

"Somewhere another river meets this one and they flow into the ocean, which is never filled. Then they sing their joy with such energy and tenderness that, up there, on his heavenly throne, God smiles down on them, and His smile throws light on us while the two rivers warm us."

Under the same impetus, they both threw two more words into the river current: "Thank you." And Haskel, who had just joined them, added, "Thank you, God; thank you, rivers; thank you, children; yes, thank you, world; thank you, Creation. Thank you to everything in and around us that makes us love life."

Luigi returns.

"I used to curse everything that surrounded me," he says. "Whether a deep philosophical thought, a medieval chant, the call of love or the beauty of a child—I met everything with a rejection as thoughtful as it was instinctive. I liked to think of myself as inquisitor and irascible judge. It wasn't justice that I was defending, but a truth that I thought was indispensable for my own survival. Before I could lucidly confront all the things that predated my appearance, I yelled: No, no, I don't want memories."

Shaltiel wonders if he should remind his torturer that he belongs to a people whose children had arguments for cursing the world that were so much more valid—that they didn't use. But the Italian is speaking again.

"I started reading in depth all the books that try to relate the unspeakable. Books by historians, by survivors. But then I read books by the 'enforcers,' in other words, the murderers. They attracted me. That's how I had the idea of joining people who, out of a strange need for purity, were contemplating destroying the world in order to save it. What once was, they believed, must no longer be. Hence, their willingness to fight. Though of the same age as the generation of 1968, I didn't join their movement. I understood their motives and had sympathy for their political-poetical dreams, but that was all. They didn't go far enough."

Once again, Shaltiel feels a drop of pity—Luigi is a victim of his father's crimes. But he doesn't deserve Shaltiel's empathy. He can't help but listen, though: After all, the truth of the opposite camp is also a truth.

Luigi goes on with his story in a voice that is tense but calm. He keeps his eyes lowered: What was he looking for on the grimy floor covered with refuse?

"Then I plunged into the works of Nechayev and Bakunin. I was attracted by the anarchist, nihilist, extremist path, obsessed by the void, the downfall and the nothingness that follow the shattering of passions and dreams. I joined the outlawed Japanese, Italian and German revolutionary groups. The Red Brigades. I met the devoted followers of Mao, Trotsky and Stalin who had aged so badly, unhinged by their denial of limits. The killers who kill while laughing. The clandestine carriers of grenades and bombs intended for any haphazardly chosen victim. Exterminating angels. Yes, my unfortunate Jewish storyteller, I have blood on my hands. But unlike my father, the blood I shed was not Jewish. However, that could happen. You have to know, you have to tell it to the good Lord of the Jews, up there, if you believe in Him: Tell Him I belong to a Palestinian terrorist cell. Can you imagine why? The terrorists think my goal is to help them drive the Jews out of their country and contribute to the creation of an Arab Palestine. They're mistaken. Their pompous and fiery discourse leaves me cold, as do all forms of nationalism and patriotism. Including that of the Jews. Weren't my father and his comrades patriots? Didn't they love the imperial, global visions of their demented leader? And what about the Germans who vowed loyalty to their Führer even after his downfall? No, I feel close to the Palestinian cause because it pushes rational terrorism across uncharted frontiers. I remembered Munich in 1972, the Olympic games and the murder of the Israeli athletes by masked Palestinian terrorists. I had the kind of presentiment that never misleads. It comes from the training I received in Palestinian bases in Lebanon, Iraq and other places. The day is not far off when suicide terrorism will be global."

The Italian is now talking in a slow monotone, as though he were reciting a text he had learned by heart. And Shaltiel listens to him with keen attention, as though he senses that his own salvation depends on it. Perhaps he also dreads Ahmed's return, for then this exchange would immediately be interrupted. And then . . .

"Not since the eleventh century, when Sheikh Hassan ibn Sabbah sent his emissaries to the four corners of Islam armed with daggers to kill their enemies and kill themselves, has the world known these kinds of revolutionary deeds. I saw how today's young soldiers—adolescents among them—were trained and for what. They were trained to die in order to kill. I'm talking about tomorrow's suicide killers of course. They'll go far, very far. The Sheikh targeted specific adversaries; future suicide terrorists will attack innocent people—strangers, women and children. If Death could die, they would be its reincarnation. That's what will be new. You've probably read

Dostoyevsky? He tells of a time in Czarist Russia when the conspirators planned the assassination of the Grand Duke for weeks. Everything was ready for a Sunday when he would be going to church. The man was already as good as dead. Except that in the last minute he decided to take his children with him, and this ruined everything—the assassins would not kill children."

Shaltiel asks: "What about you? Could you kill children in the name of your theories?"

"Me, maybe not. Ahmed, yes."

"And this doesn't appall you?"

"He's a true revolutionary. He's fighting for a sacred cause."

"And you? What cause are you fighting for?"

"Me, I'm fighting against all causes."

"But by helping Ahmed kill—kill children even—aren't you his accomplice?"

"Yes, I am. But only an accomplice. Legally it's the same thing, but I don't give a damn about laws. I don't see it as the same thing. I demand the right to give my rebellion a meaning that transcends it. My father used to attend the executions of innocent people; I might attend one today. Taking it out on the innocent is a way of denouncing the people responsible for poverty in the world, but not just that; it's also a way of exposing the weakness, fragility and uselessness of innocence. You, my unfortunate storyteller, as a Jew, you should be able to understand that."

For the first time, Shaltiel can't control his anger. Until then, in spite of all the feelings he had had—anxiety, anguish, panic, disgust, incomprehension, the sense of unreality, absurdity and despair—wrath seemed to have been overlooked; or rather, wrath had spared him. But now it cannot be denied.

"How dare you! You use Jewish suffering just to add to it! Apparently you haven't understood a thing! You criticize the miscarriages of history and heap even more ignominy on it! You call yourself an anarchist, a nihilist? You're nothing but a pathetic power-greedy adventurer! You attribute your so-called revolutionary motives to the tragedy of my people, whereas you're prepared to contribute to this tragedy through me because I'm a Jew! It's not sufficient for you that your father was guilty, that he fueled the hatred that made him important, powerful and tyrannical; you also want to resemble him! Get a grip on yourself; get rid of your mental aberrations! Snap out of your wild, falsely intellectual imaginings! You're repelled by the generation of 1968, intellectual mentors make you laugh: What are you doing in this world with its tormented, wounded memory, a world that is desperately trying to recover and comfort itself by inventing new hopes and giving itself a little bit of joy, serenity and happiness? Go away, get the hell out, and for the love of God, stop using my people in your ideological arguments—their slow death as they walked to the fires and common graves under your father's scrutiny, if not under his orders. There are limits even to blasphemy!"

Luigi is unmoved.

"Did you look through my wallet? It's there on the floor. Inside, you'll find the photo of a man in a summer shirt. Look at it! Look at his arm! You'll see the number tattooed on it. Do you know what that means?"

Luigi bends down, picks up the wallet and takes out the photo. He examines it.

"Yes," he says, "I know."

"It's my father," Shaltiel says.

. . .

One year, to the day, after having left Blanca, Shaltiel was reunited with her. She looked proud and pretty, and still tilted her head. During his entire absence, they hadn't been in touch.

Shaltiel looked back on that day with a feeling of gratitude but also of embarrassment and—why not admit it?—shame. Even for a couple in love, there are bitter pills to swallow in the course of their lifetime.

They arranged to meet under the same tree, and on the same park bench, where they had sat the last time they met. They looked at each other with the same feeling of helplessness, without kissing. As radiant as before and even more attractive, her lips slightly fuller, her eyebrows thicker, Blanca initiated the conversation in a neutral and direct tone of voice.

"You'll tell me about your trip later and I'll tell you about my studies, my work with Professor Goldmann. But, for now, I just want you to know I've remained faithful. What about you? Did you?"

"I didn't betray you," he answered. "You believe me, don't you?"

"You didn't understand my question. I asked if you've been faithful."

"Do you want to know if I thought about you all the time? All I can tell you is that I met a lot of people, asked a lot of questions, heard a lot of stories, and you were always present in my mind." He paused. "One other thing: I missed you."

She thought at length before answering, still without smiling.

"That's enough for me. And now let's speak about our love."

He sighed. "I loved you; I love you."

They kissed and then were silent for a long time, as in the past, before expressing the feelings close to their hearts. Shaltiel felt the onset of desire; she too. Nothing seemed to have changed. The park was still leafy and green; the passersby still had their worries; the sky, its color. And two youths were about to receive from each other the joy of the human truth that lights up the eternal passions of mankind.

"Listen, Shalti, I have a question that's tormenting me," Blanca said, lowering her head, and then raising it and looking at him straight in the eyes. "Did you ever wonder how we managed to love each other for so long without making love?"

Shaltiel felt a pang of anguish. "Yes, of course, I often wondered. Because, as you know, I wanted to, terribly. But I felt you didn't want to, or rather that you weren't ready."

She saw herself again as a little girl, facing her parents and their usual reproaches that were not always unfair.

"You were right. I wasn't ready."

Shaltiel felt a nascent anxiety though he couldn't fathom its origin or consequences. A doubt went through his mind: Perhaps she isn't a virgin. How could he ask her without humiliating her? Didn't she have the right to have known someone before meeting him?

She seemed to decipher his look of sadness.

"Yes, you guessed it. But it isn't what you think . . ."

Composing herself, she took a deep breath and held back her sighs before confiding in him.

She must have been thirteen years old. Going home one night after dining at a friend's house, she was brutally attacked by a stranger. He had hit her over and over again to silence her screams as he raped her. She was ashamed of going home.

Shaltiel felt anger well up in him, not against his girlfriend, but against an environment where such crimes could occur. If he saw this man in the street, would he be able to contain his rage?

"I was afraid and I was ashamed," Blanca continued. "I was afraid of what you might say or do. That's why, before, I couldn't . . ."

Shaltiel took her in his arms and whispered in her ear. "I love you for who you are: innocence itself, wounded, violated but unchanging. We'll make love often, and you'll forget the rest. Yes, I know, a woman who was once raped remains raped for life. But, in my eyes, in my soul, our love will restore your purity."

He clasped her very tightly to his chest. "I love you even more than before."

"And I'll have your children," said Blanca. "And you'll be proud of them."

He hadn't thought of children. He was well aware of what everyone thinks: Thanks to children, life becomes the finest, loveliest tale. Now, in jail, Shaltiel thought that his position had been most wise. Why give life to children when the destiny of men is in the hands of executioners?

"Read this, you stupid moron!" says Ahmed. "Your guilt here is plain. A filthy article in English: It's your own confession.

You believe in the coming of the Jewish Messiah, you say as much all the time—in other words, you deny the teachings of our Prophet."

Now the Italian whispers something to his accomplice, and they walk out without a word. I start reflecting on everything that's happened to me. I know I was abducted because I was in the wrong place at the wrong time. I won't "confess," so why do they keep humiliating me? My throat is dry and sore. I'm thirsty. I have an upset stomach. I'm dirty. A faint light comes through the basement window, up there; I feel it on my face. What does the window give out on? A courtyard? An avenue? There are ambulance sirens, tires screeching on the pavement. People are heading home, or going to work, to the office or to school. I'm in my own special time frame, time outside time.

Ahmed finally shows me the "proof," as he calls it, and smacks me for the fun of it. It's a short story entitled, ironically, "A Confession," which I published in a small journal of Ohio University. The hero, a Jew, dreams that he sees the Messiah bringing all the Jews back to Jerusalem.

"And you want me to believe this isn't anti-Muslim propaganda?" Ahmed says, shouting himself hoarse. "That you Jews aren't our fiercest enemies, merciless with regard to our holy Islam, and hated, repudiated by the Prophet and all those who believe in him?"

I tell him that the stories I tell are invented. He could easily check by looking at my other silly publications. And then he'd understand that the pages he's waving in front of my eyes are just the fruit of my imagination. I add that when the Messiah comes, he'll save the entire world from damnation, including the Muslims. Ahmed doesn't believe a word of what I say.

They blindfold me again. I don't know why, since I've already seen what they look like. And as I'm going to die . . . So it begins anew—waiting for torture, which can be almost as bad as the torture itself. In order not to think about it, I conjure up all my loved ones again. I see myself with them on the night of Yom Kippur. I bless each of them in turn. What are they doing? What was their reaction to my disappearance? They must have phoned all the hospitals and all the police stations. The media must be talking about it. Even though I'm not a famous writer, I doubt my disappearance went unnoticed.

My captors are here again and give me back my sight. Once again, Ahmed asks me to sign a letter demanding the release of the prisoners, condemning Israel. It's my one and only hope. I'm told more: My liberation depends on the liberation of his three comrades-in-arms. I say I won't sign anything. He wants to know if I'm aware of the consequences of my refusal. I say yes, I am.

Later, in Ahmed's absence, Luigi no longer wants to talk about revolutionary politics, which, he notes, should not be confused with political revolution. He no longer mentions social injustice. Now he wants to talk about friendship.

"Friendship," he says, "is what motivated me to join the Revolution." He explains that he comes from a large family—brothers, sisters, a horde of cousins—and there was no room for friends. Joining an underground group required a form of friendship.

"You may be confusing friendship and camaraderie," says Shaltiel.

"You see a difference?"

"Camaraderie can lead to friendship; friendship is never just camaraderie."

Luigi, more and more playing the good cop to Ahmed's villain, says, "Tell me about your friends."

One name, one face looms up in Shaltiel's mind: Jonathan. He feels overwhelmed by a warm wave of nostalgia. Friend, where are you at this very moment? What will you feel about our friendship if I die?

Jonathan is tall, slender, delicate, timid, fearful, generous, withdrawn. Women pursued him, but he remained faithful to his wife, Lina. They lived together, went to the theater, maintained many relationships, kissed each other tenderly, made love—without ever exchanging a sentence.

It was through Lina—a beautiful, radiant woman, not lacking in charm but stubborn and wedded to her convictions—that Shaltiel had met Jonathan. Lina had come to hear him tell stories about the experiences of imaginary beings. The gathering in the park was meant for children. She was the only adult in the audience.

"I have a husband and no children," she said. "But we like weird stories like yours. May I invite you to our house for a drink? We'll pay your fee."

He accepted. They lived in a small, nicely furnished apartment in midtown Manhattan.

"What kinds of stories would you like me to entertain you with?" Shaltiel asked.

"Any kind," said Lina. "Love stories, if possible. They always entertain me."

"And you?" he asked Jonathan.

"A story about friendship."

So he improvised two short stories. When he left, at about 11 p.m., he found an envelope in his coat pocket. Jonathan insisted on accompanying him out.

In the street, he remarked, "You must find us very strange."

Shaltiel said nothing.

"Do you often have the opportunity to talk to mutes?"

"But you're not mute, nor is your wife."

"Oh yes we are. Mute with each other."

"Since when?"

"Oh, for a long time.'

"How did it happen?"

"One night, we came home after dining at the house of some friends. Lina seemed irritated; even today, I don't know why. We had just gone to bed when she said, 'I've decided that in order to protect our love and keep it intact, we'll stop talking to each other. Why? Because one word can ruin everything. And our love means too much to me. I don't want to run the risk.' So that was that. She doesn't talk to me so she can love me more, and I don't talk to her so I won't lose her. She says a lot of things to a lot of people, but to me, nothing. And the same is true of me. So now you see what I mean; we're mute with each other. But our love gains in strength and genuineness."

"And would Lina give me the same explanation?"

"I think so. Ask her the next time."

Shaltiel and Jonathan were about to part at the subway station. As they were shaking hands Jonathan said, "May I ask you something?"

"Go ahead."

"It's an offer."

"I'm listening."

"Let's be friends."

"Why?" Shaltiel stammered.

"It would make Lina happy. It's her idea. Otherwise she wouldn't have organized this evening. She knows how important friendship is to me. Don't you think man could live without love but not without friendship?"

The following day, Shaltiel was surprised to see Lina again in his audience. She listened to his stories and waited to see him · after all the children had left.

"You told them beautiful things about friendship."

"I just told them children's stories. And I never used the word 'friendship.' "

"True enough, but I could still hear it. And so could the children. Because there are words that come through, even when they're unspoken."

She asked him what he made of the previous evening.

"You make a peculiar couple," he said.

"Peculiar in what way?"

"You believe in love but you seem to have given up on speech—you repudiate it, and I ask myself, What for?"

"You don't understand us. Suppose I tell you that the sole reason we keep silent is so as to prove that love can do without spoken words?"

"You're talking to someone who uses spoken words in his profession."

"But I'm talking about us, not you."

Shaltiel started to feel annoyed. "What do you expect from me?"

"That you come back to see us. Our silence improves in your presence."

"Your husband offered me his friendship."

"I know."

"He told you?"

"No. How could he? But I look at him and I hear it all. I know that you replied that you were going to think it over."

"That's true. His offer is far from frivolous. I have to give it thought."

This eventually led to long walks with Jonathan, to deep exchanges, to the reading of manuscripts. Blanca understood that this new friendship in her husband's life would enrich and enhance their love.

Sometimes the four of them spent evenings together—dining, attending concerts and talking about the music. They were comfortable with one another. Blanca and Shaltiel were careful not to disturb the strange, unnatural harmony that enveloped Lina and Jonathan.

"So," said Luigi, "are you going to tell me about your friends, political or otherwise?"

"I have a friend named Jonathan," says Shaltiel. "In Hebrew, 'Jonathan' means 'gift from God.' Jonathan was the best friend of the future King David in his youth."

"Friendship is a beautiful bond," said Luigi. "I admit it's a gift from God to men."

Pinhas's surprising adventures were hardly talked about in his family. When he was little, Shaltiel couldn't understand why the mere mention of his name disrupted the serenity of the household. Later on, he would learn more about how his brother had broken with tradition and was living in Russia, where he held an influential position. Many years later, in Jerusalem, he learned more, from Pinhas's own mouth.

Shaltiel was very eager to see him, because he had been told that his elder brother, who had been an exemplary Communist in his youth, had become deeply religious. He wanted to understand why. What had led him to abandon the God of his ancestors for Stalin, a god of war with a mustache, obsessed with absolute power, for whom human beings were not an ideal but a political product? And what had prompted his brother's falling out with this new master and allowed him to find his way back to the God of Abraham and Moses?

They met one summer evening in the Old City, in a small common room of a social center where impecunious yeshiva students gathered now and then to discuss politics, loans or marriage. With his bushy beard and earlocks, caftan and black felt hat, Rabbi Pinhas looked like a rabbi descended from generations of erudite rabbis.

"Hello, Pavel," said Shaltiel. "I'm so glad to see you."

"Don't call me Pavel anymore," his brother said. "My name is Pinhas."

Shaltiel wanted to ask him to explain his name change, but first he asked how someone who used to be secular could now feel fulfilled by returning to his original faith and no longer show the slightest interest in his youthful political activities.

His head lowered as if he were shielding his gaze, Pinhas explained that his coming to Israel had nothing to do with politics but with deeper needs. Shaltiel asked him to elaborate.

"I'm sure you know that for years I ministered to a temporal secular cause that was actually deceitful. At one point I understood that it was time to turn my back on it and find the way to truth again. I couldn't bear the lies, the ruses and the violence anymore. I owed it to myself to start my life over again."

Shaltiel remained silent.

"I imagine you'd like to know everything about the Communist period in my youth. They must have talked about it at home, right? How I became a Stalinist? The event, the discovery, the meeting that led to the change in my behavior and my commitment? Our father played an important part at the beginning of this adventure. You're surprised by that? Listen.

"As you know, he was always devout, very devout. And poor. He prayed morning and evening, studied the Talmud and helped the needy. If anyone deserved health, peace, happiness and the means to accomplish good deeds, it was he. Upright, honest, loyal to the Law of Moses and the prophets, he lived for us, his family, and for others just as much.

"I was still young, I worked in the sawmill and was preparing my bar mitzvah. One day, I saw him weeping in his bedroom. That day, a neighbor had come to ask him for help. Her husband was penniless; their only daughter was gravely ill; they were going to be evicted from their house. Our father could do nothing to help them. He could only offer them tears. Some time later, my friend Zelig gave me a Communist pamphlet in Yiddish. When I read it, it opened my eyes to what I believed was enlightenment. He gave me other publications. Little by little, I understood that the path chosen by our father wasn't the only path and that perhaps it wasn't even the best way of improving man's condition and fulfilling the Messianic expectation of Jews. Communism seemed to me as good if not better. It was new, original. And it offered us a way we could help improve the world, to discover the roots of evil and defeat it. Can you understand that? The slogans were more than words; the promises more than sentences. Remake humanity; build a world where children don't die of hunger, where their parents are no longer ashamed. Bearers of a pure flame, we were determined to set fire to everything that led to the misfortune of men.

"I decided to change my life. In order to take responsibility for my new life, it was incumbent on me to leave everything behind. So I left for the Soviet Union."

Pinhas glanced at his watch and realized that it was time to recite the Maariv prayer.

He asked his brother to excuse him and to wait for him to return.

·   ·   ·

On a dark, moonless night, under a sky heavy with portent, Zelig and Pavel crossed the frontier. Pishta Bàcsi, a smuggler by profession, knew every path, every tree in the mountains. He also knew which unit of the border police took which route and when. After a three-hour walk, he signaled for them to stop.

"Count twenty-three oaks on the right and you'll be on the other side," he whispered to them.

Pavel and Zelig held their breath and cautiously crawled through the humid grass for about ten minutes.

"Halt!" someone shouted in Russian.

The two friends believed they had reached *their* promised land.

The order was repeated, more menacingly. "Halt!"

Relieved to have left Romania, they were about to stand up when the same voice told them to freeze.

A flashlight shined on them. Zelig, who spoke some Russian, tried to explain to the Russian soldier.

"On your knees!'

The soldier called for help. His comrade searched the intruders. He then ordered them to the nearby guardroom.

"Why are you here? Who sent you? You've just trespassed on Soviet territory illegally."

Zelig replied with conviction that he and his friend had their red membership cards in their pockets, proving they belonged to the party of the great Stalin. The officer found the cards but was unimpressed. Documents like these could be printed by anyone, he said. He confiscated them, as well as everything the suspects had in their possession, including their money.

Handcuffed, they were led to a military truck that was standing by. Zelig tried to reassure his friend.

"Don't worry. These soldiers aren't qualified to handle our case. As soon as we're introduced to a high-ranking officer, the misunderstanding will be cleared up. I'm confident."

They spent endless hours in a jail cell. Zelig tried to convince Pavel that what was happening to them was normal, understandable. After all, they were in a military zone. In a few days, everything would be cleared up. The party would send someone to ease their path. Pavel remained doubtful. How could they prove their innocence to the Soviets?

"I trust the party," said Zelig.

Finally they were escorted, separately, to appear before a military security officer. They were asked the same questions: Why had they entered the USSR illegally? What was their objective? Who were their contacts? The two said they were members of the underground Communist party; they had decided to come to Soviet Russia quite simply to help the party triumph over its enemies.

Then the officer brought them in together.

"Did the Soviet government invite you to come to this country?"

"No. But the party's secret service . . ."

"We have no proof of this."

"But our superiors, in our town . . ."

"We don't know them. And you, do you know anyone here?"

No, no one, they said.

"Consider yourselves under arrest. If you were real Communists, you would have known that discipline prevails over everything else. It's our party, responsible for our national security, that decides which of its members are to come and help us, how and when. If you are Communists, why didn't you wait until you were summoned?"

Zelig turned to Pavel and asked, "Didn't you once tell me you had a relative in the USSR?"

"Yes, I think I do."

"Do you remember his name?"

"A cousin . . . an uncle . . ."

The officer sniggered. "What makes you think I would just happen to know this cousin or uncle or whomever?"

"I'm not sure you would know him, comrade officer," said Zelig, "but . . ."

"Watch your language! Until your identity as a party member has been verified, I forbid you to call me comrade!"

Zelig and Pavel were escorted back to their cell. The next day, they were transported north. Each night they stayed in another prison. They were hungry, exhausted, thirsty, scared, nostalgic, full of regret. Zelig clung to his ideals; Pavel was less sure.

Zelig: "Don't judge the party on the basis of what's happening to us. We're the victims of bureaucracy. Some papers must have gone astray. Don't forget that they see us as Hungarian or Romanian, in other words, as enemies of the Soviet Union."

Pavel: "But you're forgetting the Molotov-Ribbentrop Pact. We're supposed to be allies."

Zelig: "The party knows what it's doing."

Pavel: "Still, don't you wonder about the alliance between Nazis and Communists?"

Zelig: "The party has its reasons!"

Pavel: "You talk about the party the way my father used to talk about God."

Zelig: "I don't believe in God, but I believe that the Communist ideal is sacred. I hope the same goes for you."

Pavel didn't answer.

June 22, 1941.

Hitler's armies launch an all-out offensive against the Soviet Union. After a series of defeats, the Red Army needs men and equipment. Some prisoners are freed, and some of the deported are brought back from Siberia. Zelig is to enter the infantry, whereas Pavel, found to be medically unfit, is appointed to the Department of Transportation.

Desperate, Zelig urges Pavel to try again to convince the authorities of his family tie in the USSR.

"They won't believe us," says Pavel.

"It's still worth a try. What have we got to lose?"

Zelig introduced himself to a lieutenant. "Excuse me, but I think that if you're willing to listen to me, you'll see that I have something important to tell you."

"I'm listening," says the officer. "Be brief."

"My comrade Pavel's cousin works in the Kremlin," he said, standing at attention.

"Speak. I'm listening."

"He works with one of Stalin's close collaborators."

"And what's this cousin's name?"

"Meirovitch. He works with Lazar Kaganovich."

The officer gave a start.

"Bring in your friend!"

A few minutes later, Pavel introduced himself.

"I want to hear it from you," the officer said, staring at Pavel. "Is it true—you have a friend in the Kremlin?"

Trying to control his trembling, Pavel said yes, it's true.

The officer rose nervously. "Why didn't you tell us this earlier?"

Zelig, standing at the door, coughed gently, trying to intervene.

"We tried," says Zelig.

The lieutenant ignored him. "Pavel, do you realize what you're saying? Do you know that Lazar Kaganovich is among the most loyal confidants of Comrade Stalin?"

"I didn't make anything up."

Forty-eight hours later, Pavel was on his way to Moscow.

Shaltiel tries to remember how and when Pavel broke with his Communist past, reimmersed himself in his ancestral faith, retook his Jewish name Pinhas.

Did Pavel's break date from his memorable impromptu visit to the Moscow synagogue on the day of Rosh Hashanah? The visit had shaken him, that's for sure. But it hadn't caused a definitive rupture. Something else had been necessary for his life to change.

Shaltiel was present when Pavel confided in his father. He had come from Jerusalem to take part in the family celebration. It was on a Saturday afternoon, of course, at home.

Pavel and his father were meeting for the first time since the war. After the requisite small talk, there was a silence. Pinhas spoke up: "I'm thinking about Davarowsk and Moscow—they seemed so far from each other. Much farther than Moscow from Jerusalem."

"Explain what you mean," said Haskel.

"I mean, to paraphrase the great Rabbi Nachman of Breslov, that from wherever he sets off, the Jew always returns to Jerusalem." Then Pinhas started describing what he called one of the saddest episodes in his life.

"When disillusion had taken me under its wing, I talked to Leon Meirovitch about Davarowsk. He cried. He cried for the living and the dead, for his family that he would never see again. He, the staunch, die-hard Communist, entrenched in his ideology, who swore only by Marx and Lenin, Stalin and Kaganovich, cried his heart out. I quietly stood in a corner of his office. I felt indiscreet, ill at ease. 'I've betrayed them,' he whispered. 'I betrayed my poor parents and their relatives. I made them suffer when I deserted their home and tradition. I substituted my faith for theirs. I believed in a future that refuted theirs, now I realize I was on the wrong track, a track that doesn't lead to the liberation of nations but to their enslavement. It doesn't lead to the land where our people would find sovereignty, serenity and the happiness promised by the prophets of pure socialism. It leads to the camps where freezing temperatures kill the body and despair demeans the spirit. Revolutions are too bloody. Give a banner to a people and they will make it red, drenching it in their own blood and those of their martyrs, the blood of their enemies, real and imagined, as well as their victims. I have lived and fought under a delusion, for a delusion. And now it's too late to start over.' "

A short time later, when he arrived in Jerusalem, clandestinely helped by his cousin to escape the Soviet Union, in spite of his age, Haskel's eldest son went to sit on the benches of a yeshiva. This was so Pinhas could delve more deeply into Pavel's remorse.

Shaltiel recalls that Paritus had given him a brief lecture on mystical madness. Is it a powerful and implacable rebellion against linear or discursive thought? What does it seek, except to push tradition and heritage to the bottom of the abyss? Is it the rejection of what seems stable, well-founded, precise, necessary and inevitable? Finally, it is the victory of words, Paritus had said, words that find meaning in the heart.

And God is always there. He questions when He is questioned. His very silence questions. How should He be answered? Does the mystic stop being a mystic, or simply stop being, when He says no to him?

Me, I tell children about the old age that awaits them. I remind old people of their receding past.

Is it my destiny? It's my passion, I admit it. Even when I don't speak, my silence is still haunted by speech.

God himself needed to express Himself in order to undertake His oeuvre, which, afterward, would become that of men.

Facing the recesses of time and the traps of memory, entangled in pain, hope or speech, he sometimes falters, floats, trembles. Memory will always be something other than an aggregate of words, well or badly strung together. When man feels the need to throw himself into the fray, his speech changes into action.

For the good of all, I say: Be careful, the brutality of the world must not be more powerful or attractive than love and friendship. Celebrate speech instead of scorning it; elevate it to the level of prayer so that up there, the Judge of men will give men an appetite for serenity.

Life is a tale. When I was a child, this is what everyone told me; as an adult I repeated it. Sometimes it starts well and ends badly; at other times, it presages misfortune but brings jubilation.

But who is the storyteller? Who uses words in order to fill the imagination of the one who is listening to him?

It is of speech that I wish to talk, of speech that tosses the waves and moves with the mountain wind. Speech does not deny silence and does not replace it; it amplifies silence, just as silence, in turn, deepens speech.

Speech offers a sanctuary to silence, and silence protects it like a sanctuary.

Making a man reconcile life and conscience, truth and love, is a much more complex and brutal task than awakening the body to reality and the soul to fervor. Only rarely does one build on cleared, bare ground. But watch out—a building erected through speech on rotten soil is in danger of collapse at any time along with its content.

Speech gently caresses the hands of the sleeping child and slaps the face of the criminal. Speech demands a voice in order to live, in order to become a noose or a caress. Sometimes it scales the peaks at full speed; at other times it inches forward slowly, staggering, crawling. It is speech that helps the sick part with the living; and then again, it is also speech that makes death retreat.

During a brief respite, before dawn, Luigi, looking tired, takes advantage of the Arab's absence to remove Shaltiel's handcuffs and lets him rub his hands to get his blood circulating again.

"Since you say you're a storyteller," he said, "tell me a story. It will keep me awake."

"You're an odd one," he says. "Here I am suffering because of you, getting ready to die at your hands, and you're interested in hearing a story?"

"If it's a good story, with a bit of luck, you'll live an extra day," says Luigi.

"I don't believe you," Shaltiel says.

"Just talk," says Luigi. "What do you have to lose?"

"Okay," says Shaltiel. "A story will divert me too.

"Once upon a time," he began, "there was a blind king who was desperate for light in order to admire the stars. He turned to his most illustrious advisers—physicians, philosophers, artists—and promised ten thousand gold coins to the person who would help him escape the darkness, if only for an instant.

"One of them handed him a miracle-making flask inherited from his great-grandfather; another brought him a mirror that reflected hidden and invisible things; a third prayed for him, in vain. The king could see nothing.

"He was giving up hope when an old beggar introduced himself and said in a very low voice, 'Your Majesty, for a very long time I was like you, blind to the world that surrounded me. The beautiful blossoming trees, the rays of the sun, the merchants at the fair, the courtiers clustering around the wealthy—I didn't see these things. Then, in my peregrinations throughout the kingdom, I met a young woman of such radiant beauty that her gaze lit mine. Would you like me to introduce her to you? She is far away, but I know where to find her.'

" 'Of course I'd like to meet her,' said the king. 'Go get her quickly.'

"He ordered that the beggar be provided with the speediest horse-drawn coach. The old man returned a month later, empty-handed and sad.

" 'I'm sorry, Your Majesty, I arrived too late. The beautiful young woman died in a mountain accident. The entire village where she lived is in tears.'

"Downcast, the king began to cry as well.

" 'Is this the first time you're shedding tears?' asked the old beggar.

" 'Yes,' said the king. 'The very first time.'

" 'So you've never *seen* your starving subjects, their sick children, the unfortunate languishing in jail?'

" 'No, never,' said the king.

" 'Well, Your Majesty, now you know what human suffering is. You're not blind; it's that you have a heart of stone. You became indifferent to pain, poverty and the misfortune of your subjects. You forgot that each one of them—each of us—is a universe that deserves your attention and compassion. Look up into my eyes and tell yourself that my gaze contains the light that shone in the eyes of the beautiful young woman who has passed away.'

"A minute later, the king saw him and embraced him. And the entire kingdom celebrated the old beggar's wisdom."

"And what's the moral of this story?" the Italian asked. "Am I supposed to guess it?"

Shaltiel took his time too before answering.

"I think you've already guessed it."

And, at that moment, for the first time, Shaltiel began to feel a glimmer of hope.

Shaltiel's father was right. The powerful world of Jewish history also manifests itself on the individual level. Yes, Pavel had a cousin at the Kremlin. Yes, his cousin worked with Lazar Kaganovich.

Pavel spent several weeks in a detention center in a Moscow suburb. The conditions there were more tolerable than in a GPU prison. All the prisoners were waiting for their cases to be settled. There was tension because the Socialist homeland was at war. The front was moving closer. The Red Army was losing thousands of men every day. Cities were falling with breathtaking speed. The entire country was mobilizing, arming itself. Long-standing political prisoners and new offenders volunteered to fight under the red banner. Officers were freed from the Gulag to fight.

One morning, they came for Pavel. An officer, at his desk, looked through a thick file and checked his identity. The officer gestured to his assistant with a conspiratorial look and, without a word, the latter invited the former prisoner to follow him. Outside, a military car was waiting. They were on the road for three hours, driving through obstacles and barricades, and going through checkpoints where his escort had to show documents to suspicious inspectors and scrupulous soldiers. Not one word was exchanged in the car. Pavel wondered where he was being taken and for what reason. He didn't dare ask a question.

On arriving at the Kremlin, the escorting officer remained outside and another officer took over, after submitting Pavel to cross-examination and a thorough frisking. They made their way through corridor after corridor until they stood in front of a huge desk cluttered with newspapers and documents. A civilian with a mustache who sat behind the desk held out his hand and smiled.

"So, my dear relative, here you are," said Leon Meirovitch. Guessing Pavel spoke no Russian, he greeted him in Yiddish.

"So it's true?" said Pinhas.

"What?"

"True that I have a cousin in the Kremlin?'

"Why wouldn't it be true?"

"For a Communist like me, it's . . ."

"Utopian? Please, sit down."

Pavel complied. He gazed about: There was a huge portrait of Stalin and a photo of Stalin at a younger age, with Lenin. On the desk, another, smaller picture showed a man in his forties, with broad shoulders, a beaming face and piercing eyes. Who could it be? His cousin guessed his question and answered.

"It's the man I work for, Lazar Kaganovich. Have you heard of him?"

"Yes. A childhood friend, a Communist Jew like me, told me wonderful things about him. Is he really so close to Stalin?"

"Yes he is. Who is this friend?"

Pavel told him about Zelig and his devotion to the party,

and of all their adventures. That Zelig was being detained. "He's the person who got me to join the party," said Pavel.

His cousin smiled. "In that case, I owe him a debt of gratitude. If not for him, I wouldn't have met you. I'll look into his situation."

They talked about relatives and friends. Leon told him the Germans were massacring Jews by the thousands. The tragedy of Babi Yar in Kiev was the most recent slaughter. In several cities and villages they had locked Jews into synagogues and set them on fire. Pavel suspected the Germans were persecuting Jews in the lands they occupied, but such atrocities were far beyond his imagination.

"And what about Davarowsk?" he asked.

"No news for the time being. The city is occupied by the Hungarians. As for you, Pavel, you're going to stay with me. You'll live at my house, take Russian courses and work for me. Does that suit you? You should know that our office is part of the security service. So, is it yes?"

"Yes," said Pavel. "But may I remind you please not to forget my friend Zelig."

"I've made a note of it." (His intercession would come too late—Zelig died at the front.)

Yesterday a prisoner in the Gulag, today an employee in the Kremlin.

Thanks to his job, Pavel became closer with the Yiddish-speaking Jewish poets and writers Peretz Markish, Dovid Bergelson, Der Nister and Itzik Pfeffer, and even the great actor Solomon Mikhoels. In his position as Kaganovich's official representative, he attended all their meetings, parties and lectures. He was introduced to Ilya Ehrenburg, the distinguished Soviet journalist, equally at home in Paris and Moscow. Markish recited his war poems to him, praising the courage of Jews in the face of disaster. Der Nister told him about the renowned Rabbi Nachman of Breslov.

After Germany was defeated, he succeeded in convincing his cousin to invite Lazar Kaganovich to come with them to see the renowned actor Solomon Mikhoels perform at the Moscow State Jewish Theater. When Kaganovich appeared in the special box reserved for the most important Kremlin personalities, a buzz went through the audience. The spectators rose and applauded him as though a great hero were standing before them.

After the performance, a dinner was organized with Mikhoels and the actors. They discussed the news from Palestine, where underground movements were resisting British oppression.

Kaganovich boasted of his friendship with Stalin. It was he who had overseen the building of the bunker for the Little Father of the People during the war; he who had been in charge of the trains that brought food to Leningrad during the siege. Kaganovich said that Stalin personally supported the struggle for a sovereign Jewish state in Palestine, and that Molotov, the foreign minister, was going to make a speech to that effect at the United Nations. It seemed the situation of the Jews in Russia was certainly going to improve.

Lazar Kaganovich, calm, intelligent, a good listener, was friendly with Molotov and his Jewish wife, Pauline (who loved to express herself in Yiddish), and with Beria, the KGB chief. It was said that Stalin was the only person to tease Kaganovich about his Jewish origins. Others might have wanted to, but they didn't dare.

The crowd has filled the great synagogue on Arkhipova Street, suddenly too small and narrow to accommodate it. It is Rosh Hashanah. For believers, it is the day when the Judge of peoples examines their behavior and dispenses His approval or disapproval from on high. Whose stature will be elevated and whose will be lowered? Who will live and who will die? Rosh Hashanah is devoted to meditation and prayer, in other words, to everything that belongs to the spiritual in human beings.

But this crowd is not here for that reason. It is here to welcome Jews from a faraway, sun-filled country. For the first and only time, the official representative of the new state of Israel, Mrs. Golda Meirson (changed to Meir), has decided to come to the synagogue with her circle of advisers. She comes not as a practicing Jew, but simply because she is Jewish. She wants to meet her formerly invisible brothers and sisters.

Not far away, Leon Meirovitch steps into Pavel's office.

"Let's take a little walk. Get some air. It's such a beautiful day."

Pavel nods his head approvingly.

"Today is Rosh Hashanah," Leon says. "Did you forget?"

"No," says Pavel, "I didn't."

"Before leaving Davarowsk, did you go to synagogue?"

"Yes. With my parents."

"Even after becoming a Communist?"

"Yes, even then. First, because I didn't want them to find out. Secondly, I love liturgical songs. I also wanted to be with my people."

"Well, today I feel that way. Let's go to the synagogue. After all, that's also part of our duties: keeping an eye on the minorities."

Arkhipova Street was deserted. Lit by several suspended candelabras, the synagogue was far from full: several dozen old men, the frail and aged cantor and the rabbi with his white beard, were swaying to the rhythm of the prayers. Pavel and his cousin find seats. Soon all the seats were taken. Pavel asks a young man, "What's happening?"

"The Israeli diplomats are here. There they are, up there, in the balcony."

Leon and Pavel hear a commotion outside and go to look. They can't believe their eyes: the crowd was as large as on May 7 on Red Square. They elbow their way through. It is as if every Jew in the city has decided to take part in an event whose full meaning they do not grasp. But they sense its importance.

Leon and Pavel are stunned. They've never witnessed anything like this scene; they had no idea there were so many Jews in Moscow, or that they were so bold in flaunting their Jewishness.

"If God is looking down on us," says Pavel, "He's surely proud of his people."

"Unfortunately, he's not the only one looking," Leon replies.

From that day on, Leon is no longer the same man. He seems worried most of the time and closets himself in his office to brood.

One day, Pavel says to him, "Your mood worries me. What is it that so preoccupies you? Is it me? Am I doing my job badly?"

Leon reassures him. It has nothing to do with Pavel. He invites him to dinner, not at home, but in a restaurant; not the one for the privileged officials, but a brasserie that he goes to occasionally.

On the way, he says in a low voice, "You were right about Lazar Kaganovich. He *is* Jewish. Well, he was with Stalin in his dacha in Kuntsevo when Beria delivered his report on the 'gigantic demonstration'—his expression—the Moscow Jews organized in front of the synagogue. Stalin reacted angrily, accusing the Jews of every conceivable crime—insufficient loyalty to the regime, connections with hostile intelligence services, espionage for Israel, hence America, hence the enemies of the Soviet Union. He ordered Beria to take measures. Kaganovich is too high up in the party hierarchy; he won't be touched. But I'm vulnerable. And who knows what trouble they could make for us Jews. Beria is capable of anything."

"What can we do? Couldn't Kaganovich explain to comrade Stalin . . ."

"That Jews aren't spies? That half a million Jews wore the Red Army uniform? That a great number were killed in action? That many were decorated as heroes of the Soviet Union? Stalin knows all this, but he tends to see conspiracies everywhere. Don't forget, Trotsky and Kamenev and Zinovyev—many other influential party officials were Jewish."

"Are you worried?"

"Yes. I've never seen Kaganovich so preoccupied."

Little by little, measures are taken against some Jews. There are sudden disappearances and suspects arrested. Solomon Mikhoels is murdered in Minsk. Then comes the liquidation of the Jewish Antifascist Committee made up of distinguished Jewish personalities from the literary, social and political worlds. More arrests, indictments, deportations and death sentences follow. Jewish clubs, organizations and publications are ordered shut. Jewish printing houses are destroyed. The press begins to carry anti-Semitic propaganda. Jews are beginning to panic, though, of course, they don't dare show it.

Leon and Pavel are aware of the situation but don't know how to deal with it. In whom can they confide their pain and anxiety? It seems wiser to wait and see.

One fall afternoon, Leon tells Pavel he is arranging for him to leave Moscow.

"The situation is getting worse. I can't do anything for myself; they'll arrest me if I request an assignment abroad. But I can get you out, on a diplomatic visa."

Pavel is speechless. But he sees Leon is leaving him no choice. The Soviet bureaucracy is disorganized enough for him to have a chance of succeeding. But what will become of Leon? He will certainly pay a price for granting freedom to his subordinate. Does Pavel have the right to expose him to this danger?

Pavel spends several sleepless nights. He has to make a decision. Time was short. Leon tells him several times that the situation is deteriorating. Stalin requires all high-ranking government figures, Jewish or not, to sign a virulent anti-Jewish letter. Most of the Jews obeyed. Not Kaganovich, though he knew his own life was at stake.

"The ax is aiming higher and higher," says Leon to Pavel. "They now have Kaganovich in their sights. Whatever you decide to do, do it fast."

Ahmed, his face bathed in sweat, frothing with rage, shouts at
Shaltiel.

"They're all sons of bitches! Cursed infidels! They refuse
to negotiate! For four days and four nights, we've done everything to taunt them and frighten them, to show them that we're
capable of anything to defeat them. But those Yid bastards and
their American pals, all enemies of Islam, refuse to listen to us.
They refuse to negotiate. They're prepared to let this idiot here
die. What will our brothers think of us? That we're incompe-
tent! Or cowards!"

"Calm down," Luigi says to him. "The die isn't cast yet.
There's no sense in getting all worked up. Let's think this thing
through. We still have our hostage. What if we offer to let
him go?"

"You're joking," said Ahmed, trying to control his rage.
"The terrorist has only one choice. He must be strong. He must
strike, to set an example for the future."

"Yes, but so far in this case it's led nowhere."

"With these damned infidels, only hatred, brutal force and
a gruesome death will make them bend."

Shaltiel knows he's the victim of a political negotiation gone
bad. His breathing quickens. His heart is racing. It's the end, he
thinks. Ahmed is determined to liquidate him. He can't take the
risk of giving Shaltiel his freedom; he would provide a descrip-
tion that would immediately enable the police experts to sketch
his portrait, which would instantly be distributed throughout
the world. No, his time is running out.

If it is true that the soul and consciousness, before taking leave, relive everything that contributed to a life, he would like his memories to be whole, true, authentic. The important thing for him is not to forget anything. The spiderweb up there on the right side of the sooty ceiling, the mosquito crawling on his left arm—these details require clarity.

A Talmudic saying comes to his mind. On the first day of the funeral, the dead person hears an angel who comes to his tomb, knocks and asks his name. Woe to the one who forgets it.

Don't forget, don't forget, Shaltiel mumbles to himself. Shaltiel, son of Haskel and Miriam, don't forget.

A Talmudic Sage said that when the soul is led before the celestial court, the first thing it is supposed to prove is that it has always been honest in its dealings with its fellow men. What about me? Shaltiel wonders feverishly. What will I say about my work and obsessions? Did I earn my living honestly? Did I make words lie to make them acceptable? How is one to detect the truth in lies?

The people of his life and journey define him.

He is overcome by a strange need for tenderness. Dorothea the governess smiles at him. The count looks at him with kindness. His father hands him the ancient manuscript that was the pride and treasure of his life, saying, "I entrust it to you so that you'll give it to Rabbi Hayim Vital." Blanca opens her arms to him. Paritus asks him a question in a whisper; it's the second question the soul is supposed to answer: Did you hope for Redemption?

Redemption: Is Shaltiel still waiting for it? Is it for the Jewish people whose destiny and faith are defined by a timeless expectation, waiting for the one who puts off coming to save them, Shaltiel and the entire world?

He sees Blanca again as a young woman, in love and loved, radiant and happy. How did they come so close to breaking up? Why did they never have a child? And now, how will she react to his death?

He sees his parents again. They will be shattered, irreparably. He is their joy, their pride. The only future they have left. Sprawled out on his tomb—if he's found, which isn't at all certain—they'll grieve in silence. His father will recite the Kaddish. The Talmud again: "Woe to the generation in which the parents bury their children." His friends will weep over him. Who will tell the children stories? Though a stranger to the horrors his father witnessed, he feels tied to those, parents and grandparents, who lived through it. Should the tortured say everything or say nothing? The ultimate suffering is that he will leave no heir.

Shaltiel stiffens. He hears his torturers discuss his execution. It's as if they were deciding on a meal or choosing a restaurant. All of a sudden, the discussion gets heated. The whispers become impatient and aggressive. Luigi opposes the execution. Ahmed loses his temper. Luigi remains calm.

Ahmed: "His life puts us in danger."

Luigi: "His death even more so."

Ahmed: "I'm happy to be a martyr."

Ahmed goes to make a last phone call to Beirut, to their superiors. When he returns, everything will be settled.

For Shaltiel the tension is unbearable. A long Jewish lineage dating back for centuries will come to an end with me, he thinks. Forever.

Thursday afternoon. It's been more than eighty hours since the beginning of this affair, and Saul Rothman, the police commissioner's deputy, reports they are closing in on the abductors of Shaltiel Feigenberg.

The White House is kept informed. The exhausted family anxiously waits. The police headquarters are besieged by the media. The Israeli consulate is in constant direct phone contact with the government in Jerusalem, and, in Israel too, the public is following the events closely.

The turning point came when the Mossad announced they had succeeded in identifying the abductors as belonging to a small ultra-extremist group of fanatics with headquarters in Beirut. All the Palestinian terrorist movements operating outside the Middle East receive their orders from their leaders stationed in Syria or Lebanon. Armed with this information, the FBI and the CIA mobilized informers and wiretapped appropriate telephone lines. They discovered the abductors were somewhere in Brooklyn.

Saul's men undertook a search, district by district, street by street. Saul says, "There has been terrorist infiltration into the

Muslim communities. Sympathizers may have knowledge of the affair."

A colleague suggests the Symbionese Liberation Army may well be involved, but the police commissioner, John Ryan, says he doesn't want to widen the investigative circle too much. He trusts the information they have received; it's reliable.

"The important thing," he says, "is preventing them from murdering the hostage at the last minute."

Of course, no one can be sure of anything. The lessons from the past, though far from unanimous, are nevertheless pessimistic. More than once, police interventions have ended with the death of the abductors—and the death of their hostages. One must be patient and seize the opportunity.

A Mossad liaison asks Ryan, "What do we know about what is happening in the Muslim community? How is it reacting?"

"It's okay," says Ryan. "Lots of people condemn hostage taking on principle."

The discussion is interrupted by the appearance of an excited policeman.

"We know where they are. It's an old furniture warehouse, a three-story building with sealed windows. The two owners are students. We're checking on them now. Sounds like they might be fronts."

Outside, it is beginning to get dark.

*"You're a storyteller. Why don't you say anything about your experience
as a hostage?" The first hours, the last ones, the confrontations with the
torturers—what was it like?*

Everyone around the table is quizzing Shaltiel.

*"Tell us, what was it like from the inside? What did your thoughts
revolve around, and around whom? What about the kidnappers? Why
don't you tell us anything about them, their personalities, their behavior?
Which of the two men worried you more? Which one was most brutal,
least human? Which one would have made you break down? And after
how much time?"*

Blanca with her happy smile and his relieved parents; the police personnel involved—they are all entitled to consideration in my life and my memory, each in his own way, and now they are all trying to make me talk. Rachel, who had come from Israel to help in the investigation, asks: "Why do you refuse to confide in us?"

Should I answer that, yes, it was thanks to them, to their being there, that I was able to hold out. And thanks to my memories too. In spite of the fear and torture?

Will the person who has never been tortured ever know the solitude of the hostage, his humiliations, his incomprehension, his doubts?

How, why and to whom should I say this?

Saul explains: "In the end, we were lucky. They had no real plan. They didn't know how to improvise. They didn't show great intelligence. We were able to surprise them. Of course, killing is easy, so easy. Anyone can dispatch a life. And those two bastards were prepared to kill Shaltiel—that's obvious. But the operation itself was amateurish. They had never taken proper precautions."

He turned to Shaltiel. "You'd probably like to know more about the final act. Night had already fallen. Our preparations took less than half an hour. Our sharpshooters, negotiators and assault units encircled the warehouse.

Hagai, the Israeli liaison, said: "The operation was well prepared and well carried out. The police handled the abductors, while we focused on you. The surprise was total. We picked up Ahmed in the street; he was returning from a nearby telephone booth and was about to open the door to the warehouse. He didn't have time to shoot. Or even to shout. It was all over in a flash." *→ social issue*

This whole operation, Shaltiel thought, which was to be the crowning achievement of Ahmed's grandiose dreams, was merely a race to death. Now he had joined the "martyrs" in the Muslim paradise. There is one less murderer in the world but does it make it any better? Does it change anything? And will his children become avengers like their father? Will the chain of violence be passed on from one generation to the next? Will it never come to an end?

"The Italian is in jail, by the way," says Ryan. "Do you have anything you want to tell us, Mr. Feigenberg?"

Shaltiel thinks to himself, What will ensue? His mind is unsettled. Yesterday, he was about to die, and now . . . A distant tale, not even remotely connected, comes to mind: An odd vagabond becomes crazed with love. He loves the passersby, the houses, the trees, the clouds; he is brimming with love. Until the evening when he meets a young woman who asks him to walk her home for she is afraid of walking alone. When they reach her house, she plants a kiss on his cheek and says, "You'll remember, won't you?" That's the end of the story.

He was overawed by the last minutes of the drama, so different from the others. As the end approached, any second everything could be won or lost. The atmosphere was oppressive, the light pale—until the police burst in.

The final connection: How can it be defined? Luigi and Shaltiel had confronted each other. One incarnated strength and shame, the other nostalgia and memory. The photo of Shaltiel's father had left a mark on Luigi; he could see his pain and feel his anger. Did he grasp the dreadful message being conveyed, the cruel irony of fate? A killer was about to do to Shaltiel what his father had done to Haskel. Luigi and Shaltiel would remain isolated and in opposition, each in his camp, each in his more or less freely chosen condition, Shaltiel's of suffering and Luigi's of decline.

Can man change the way he sees others like a snake changes its skin? Could it really be true, therefore, that every human being alternates between feeling the attraction of good and curiosity about evil? A trace of Cain, and in parallel, another, sometimes conflicting, trace of Abel? What's the point of reflecting on this now? Doesn't death erase all questions about life?

Ahmed would soon reappear, thought Shaltiel. He, for one, has not changed; the fanatic is immunized against all change. The killer wants blood. To serve death. He will arrive armed with hatred, as before, as always. Determined. It's in his nature.

Linked to his bent conception of the mission vested in him by Islam. If the result of this operation turns out to be pitiful, may Death triumph at least.

Shaltiel did not know he still had to get ready for the denouement. It is believed that fear, like surprise, wanes. But not fear of the final suffering. Between two fits of terror, the condemned man still wonders whether he'll really die. If yes, why? Milena Jesenská was convinced that her friend Franz K. died from too much lucidity. And Shaltiel? From too much of what? Do all those who are about to die ask themselves these sorts of questions?

For the first and probably last time in his life, he suddenly had a vision of the hereafter. Huge crowds awaited him; he was moved by their calm composure. They had come to welcome him. Old people and adolescents, beautiful women and plain elderly ones, bearded men and clean-shaven men, some faces smiling, others melancholic—they all had agreed to be present for his arrival. Then a thought went through his agitated mind: As opposed to my father and Arele, and so many others, I will not abandon them, I will not return alone.

Luigi springs close to Shaltiel and quickly starts to free his wrists and ankles. Shaltiel doesn't react; he doesn't understand what is going on. Why does he suddenly let me loose? Shaltiel asks himself. What for? Where is he going to take me?

When Shaltiel stands up, he teeters. He's not used to it anymore. His legs are numb. Luigi holds him up. Gently, cautiously, he helps him take a few steps. They walk toward a hidden door, all the way in the back of the hideaway. Luigi opens it, checks outside and says in a low voice: "Careful on the stairs. Above, go to the right. You'll see an avenue. At this time of day, it's busy. You'll be safe."

"But why . . . how come? What about Ahmed?" Shaltiel asks foolishly. "What's he going to do? And you? You'll be punished . . . "

"Don't worry about me.

"All this is for your father," he said, and walked off into the night. *(→ The sins of the father redeemed by the sun)*

Shaltiel thanks all the guests around the table for their presence, for having been there all along; he says thank you for having freed him, for having restored his concern for dignity, for having rallied around Blanca. Blanca, even on this day of liberation, looks sad and melancholic.

Her sadness reminds him of the things they found out about each other and their inner selves. Their bitter arguments about having a child. He was afraid. Having lived through what he had lived through, he no longer trusted history or humanity. Blanca would answer, "You're forgetting that even in the ghettos, and later in the camps for displaced persons, Jews continued to love one another, become engaged, marry and have children. On the eve of being evacuated, they gambled on the future, vowing to stay united for eternity. If your parents had had the same thoughts as you, there would have been no love between us. We would have missed out on a great experience."

Shaltiel, overcome with remorse, thinks to himself: I have been foolish and irresponsible. Children, that was the problem that remains. Was it because we grew apart that we didn't have children? No, of course not.

He could see it now. He looked at Blanca with newfound tenderness; a dazzling white light was in front of him.

I was mistaken, he thinks. It isn't because we grew apart that we don't have children; it is because we don't have children that our estrangement was possible, if not inevitable. Will the terrorists have had the last word? When I die one day, will it be without heirs?

Shaltiel looks at his father, his cousins, his friends. He thinks of the person missing at the table. He'll find the words to tell Blanca that his convictions have changed.

"Mysticism gone astray is more dangerous than heresy," Shaltiel says.

"Who are you referring to?" asks Rachel.

"To my abductors."

"I understand," says Ryan.

"The Italian is in jail, you say," says Shaltiel.

"Yes, of course," says Saul. "He's being questioned. It's essential for us to find out everything about his accomplices, here, everywhere. He'll be tried, of course."

Shaltiel takes a deep breath and says, "I'd like to attend the trial."

"Of course," says Saul. "You're the most important witness in the case."

Shaltiel nods his head. "Yes, I will testify. I want to express my gratitude."

Blanca is the only one to smile at him.

Elie Wiesel was fifteen years old when he was deported to Auschwitz. He became a journalist and writer in Paris after the war, and since then has written more than fifty books, fiction and nonfiction, including his masterwork, *Night,* a major best seller when it was republished recently in a new translation. He has been awarded the United States Congressional Gold Medal, the Presidential Medal of Freedom, the rank of Grand-Croix in the French Legion of Honor, an honorary knighthood of the British Empire and, in 1986, the Nobel Peace Prize. Since 1976, he has been the Andrew W. Mellon Professor in the Humanities at Boston University.

A NOTE ON THE TYPE

The text of this book was set in Bembo, a facsimile of a typeface cut by Francesco Griffo for Aldus Manutius, the celebrated Venetian printer, in 1495. The face was named for Pietro Cardinal Bembo, the author of the small treatise entitled *De Aetna* in which it first appeared. Through the research of Stanley Morison, it is now generally acknowledged that all old-style type designs up to the time of William Caslon can be traced to the Bembo cut.

The present-day version of Bembo was introduced by the Monotype Corporation of London in 1929. Sturdy, well-balanced and finely proportioned, Bembo is a face of rare beauty and great legibility in all of its sizes.

Composed by North Market Street Graphics,
Lancaster, Pennsylvania

Printed and bound by Berryville Graphics,
Berryville, Virginia

Designed by Soonyoung Kwon